Giselle & Dro
Giving My Heart to A Boss
Written By: Nikki Nicole

Acknowledgments

What's up y'all. It's been a minute since y'all heard from me. Every book that I pen, I'll write acknowledgments. My supporters are everything to me. I may not know each one of you, if I haven't found you yet, because I will find you. Make it your business to find me. I appreciate each one of you for supporting me. Thank you for believing in me.

When I started writing, I wanted to write something different. I got tired of reading the same story lines. Every female isn't weak, and every female isn't strong. In this industry it's about trends and writing what sells. I understand the business aspect of it.

I'm not trying to follow the trend. I'm writing because, I have a lot to say, even if it's not trending. I write to inspire and motivate. I want to touch souls with my words. I'm writing for the average women, who's going through something. I want my words and stories to help you figure it out and find your way back. It's gets greater later. Believe in yourself and invest in yourself. Be your own cheerleader. I'm your cheerleader, I'm rooting for you.

Book 9 is special to me. One thing about time, you get better with time. Giselle and Dro were a pleasure to pen. You were first introduced to Dro and Giselle, in the

Journee & Juelz series. I always loved Giselle, it was something about her. I have a soft spot for her. She didn't shut down on me, one time while telling her story. She's always been open to let me do certain things.

Dro oh my, I loved him in the Baby I Play for Keeps series. I can write about him all day. I love, the way he loves Giselle. His character is different from any other male character I've wrote about. I hope y'all enjoy this stand-alone.

It's time for my **S/O Samantha, Tatina, Asha, Shanden (PinkDiva), Padrica, Chamyka, Darletha, Trecie, Quack, Shemekia, Toni, Amisha, Shonnique, Tamika, Valentina, Troy, Pat, Crystal C, Crystal L, Missy, Angela, Shelly, Lacresha, Latoya, Reneshia, Charmaine, Dominque, Ayesha, Misty, Toy, Chanta, Jessica, Snowie, Tay B, Jessica, Danetta, Blany, Neek, Sommer, Cathy, Karen, Lamaka, Bria, Kelis, Lisa, Tina, Talisha, London, Iris, Nicole, Koi, Haze, Dacha, Drea, Rickena, Saderia, Chanae, Chenelle, Shanise, Nacresha, Diamond, Tamika H, Kendra, Meechie, Avis, Lynette, Pamela, Antoinette, Crystal G, Crystal W, Wakesha, Destinee, Daerelle, Ivee, Kimberly, Kia, Yutanzia, Seanise, Chrishae, Demetria, Jennifer, Shatavia, LaTonya, Dimitra, Kellissa, Jawanda, Renea, Tomeika, Catherine** If I named everybody I will be here all day. Put your name here_____ if I missed you. The list goes on S/O to every member in my reading group, I love y'all to the moon and back. These ladies right here are a hot mess, I love them to death. They go so hard about these books it doesn't make any sense. Sometimes, I feel like I should run and hide.

If you're looking for us meet us in Nikki Nicole's Readers Trap on Facebook we are live and indirect all day.

S/O to My Pen Bae's **Ash ley**, **Chyna L**, **Chiquita**, **Misha**, **T. Miles**, **Saja Jay** I love them to the moon and back head over to Amazon and grab a book by them also.

To my new readers I have three complete series available

Baby I Play for Keeps Series 1-3

For My Savage, I Will Ride or Die Series

He's My Savage, I'm His Ridah

Journee & Juelz 1-3

Join my readers group **Nikki Nicole's Readers Trap on Facebook**

Follow me on **Facebook Nikki Taylor**

Follow me on **Twitter WatchNikkiwrite**

Like my Facebook Page **AuthoressNikkiNicole**

Instagram **@WatchNikkiwrite**

GoodReads **@authoressnikkinicole**

Visit me on the web authoressnikkinicole.com

email me *authoressnikkinicole@gmail.com*

Join my email contact list for exclusive sneak peaks. *http://eepurl.com/czCbKL*

Here's a little something for you guys Giselle & Dro playlist on Apple Musichttps://itunes.apple.com/us/playlist/giselle-dro/pl.u-e98lkMEf9X6Nbo

Contents

Giving My Heart to A Boss…

Chapter 1

<u>Giselle</u>

I've been back in the states for over a month now. I'm cool with how everything played out. I'm still standing despite everything that I've endured the past couple of months. Depression is real; I've been going through it. I've been trying to keep it together for the sake of my daughter, and what little sanity that I do have left. I wanted to see a therapist, but I've been through so much and some parts of my life I'm not ready to disclose. Time heals all wounds and, I'm praying to God that He heals a few wounds of these I have back together. I'm barely hanging on.

Coming back home and staying in this house is doing something to me. I just wanted to fucking scream. It reminds me so much of Free. I'm able to hide my feelings and breakdowns when Kassence isn't around. Free had a lot of shit with him, but despite the past month in a half, he was all I knew for a very long time. I would never wish anything bad on my child's father.

I wasn't moving out of this house at all. Free had this house built from the ground up, and it was paid for. I'm only responsible for taxes and utilities. I had to get rid of everything that reminded me of him. His scent and all his clothes, shoes, and jewelry. The family pictures that hung in the living room.

Kassence asks about him all the time. She tried to call his phone, and of course, it's no answer. No time is the perfect time to tell your daughter that her father is deceased. I'll have this conversation with her sooner than later. Today wasn't the day though. I'll be strong for her when the time comes. She looks up to me and watches me. I want her to better than me.

I went out on a few dates with Dro I was feeling it, but I wasn't. He was attractive and very handsome. Everything about him screamed boss, but I wasn't ready to give my heart to him. I've been avoiding his calls, and text for the past few weeks.

I guess he finally got the hint and stopped calling. I had too much baggage that I need to get rid of on my own. Dating isn't part of the plan right now. If it's meant to be eventually will run back into each other and, it'll happen.

I understood everything that Momma Edith was saying, but I couldn't take any more pain and heartache.

I'm not ready to date. For the past eight years, my life was built on a lie.

Snake was a mistake; he was my first before Juelz. Right after he went to prison I met Juelz; we started dating instantly. The signs were there that he was a mistake, but I ignored them. Free was a mistake. Also he gave me the greatest gift, he could ever give me Kassence, and I don't regret her at all.

I don't want to jump into something so soon. I know time heals all wounds, but mine are still fresh. My Porsche truck finally arrived from Ethiopia. Inside of the glove department and headrest. It was 100,000 in cash stuffed inside with a bag of pills. Momma Edith did exactly what she said she would do. Even in death, this man still surprised me.

I cut my music on and started cleaning my room. I started replacing the sheets and boxing up all Free's stuff. I'm keeping his jewelry and some of his designer stuff. When I open my boutique, I'll sale his stuff. Removing Free's stuff I can feel like some of the depression is being lifted.

"Mommy, what are you doing with daddy's stuff?"

"Kassence, come here baby and let me explain something to you." I took a seat on my bed. I sat Kassence on my lap I laid her head up against my chest. I stroked her little face. I began to explain to her that father is no longer with us.

She started crying I had to wipe her tears, no matter what Free did to us these past few months she loved him. I knew she would ask what was going on once I started packing his stuff up. I felt a little better since I told her that he was no longer with us. I didn't say that he was dead, but he wouldn't be coming back.

"Mommy, he doesn't love us anymore?"

"Kassence he still loves us, never question that. He just chose to not come back home with us."

"What did I do wrong?"

"Baby you didn't do anything wrong. You did everything right, sometimes people just grow apart, and they get tired of each other, so that's what happened to us." This child of mine is too smart she's probing. I hope this answer would suffice.

She got up off my lap and kissed me on my forehead and headed back to her room. Thank you, Jesus. I continued to clean my room after I finish I'll take my baby out for dinner. I hired a few contractors to come in and paint. Free's scent wouldn't leave with candles burning. Only paint and new fixtures would replace it.

***

Four hours later and I'm tired as a skunk. I really didn't feel like going anywhere, but I didn't lay out anything to cook. Kassence loves when I cook, but tonight wasn't the night. I took a hot shower and threw on some distressed jeans and an oversized Oatmeal sweater, with my Timberland booties. Kassence had a dress to match my sweater. I made sure she had thick tights underneath it was freezing outside.

I made us some reservations at Legal Seafood; it's a nice spot. I wanted to come back here since Dro met me here. I love the food and the atmosphere. Kassence and I were both ready, the drive was about forty minutes from my house. The parking lot was full. I found a parking spot that wasn't too bad. It'll take a few minutes for us to walk toward the entrance.

We finally made our way toward the entrance. I gave the hostess our name, and she showed us to our table.

"Hi, Mr. Dro." I had to do a double take to see who Kassence was speaking too. I looked up, and it was Dro, and he was with another female. Damn does he bring everybody here? I couldn't even be mad because I started ignoring him first. He looked at me, and I looked at him. I wasn't even about to speak.

"Hi Kassence, Hi Giselle." We said hi back and kept it moving. I was little pissed, and I'm sure he could sense that. Oh well, it is what it is. If he was different like, he claims. He has a funny way of showing it.

"Mommy is that Mr. Dro's girlfriend?"

"I don't know Kassence."

"Okay, mommy." The waiter sat down the menu. I ordered our drinks and food. Between Kassence asking me a million questions and seeing Dro with someone else. Instantly my mood changed from feeling great to pissed off. I had to get back focused.

I refuse to let any nigga dictate my feelings and play with my heart again. I dusted my shoulders off. Dro was sitting two tables back from us. I could feel him staring a hole in me. If you're with her than why are you looking at me, my phone went off and alerted me that I had a text. It was from him.

Dro- It ain't what it seems

I laughed, I'm sure he heard me. Why did he feel the need to explain? We just went out on three dates that's it. Nothing more nothing less.

"Mommy, what's so funny?"

"Nothing baby just a text from your grandmother," I swear she gets nosier by the hour. The waiter brought our food out. I said grace, and we began to eat. Dro and his date walked passed us. Ole girl mean mugged me as she walked by, but it's not what I think okay.

I continued to eat my food. I finished before Kassence. I checked my social media pages nothing was popping. My favorite author **Ash Ley** released the final installment to **You Ain't The Only One Trying to Be the Only One**. Tonight would be the perfect night to finish that.

Dro

Giselle ain't even my girl and feel like I've cheated. I was trying to pursue her, but she just cut a nigga off like it was nothing. My texts and phone calls would both go unanswered. I moved on and stopped hitting her up. Why did she have to be here tonight? I'm the one that brought her to this spot. Miasha wasn't shit to me. We were on a date and Netflix, and Chill was next. I planned on smashing right after we ate. I'm glad she drove I can't even get my dick wet tonight.

"Dro, are you coming?"

"No Miasha, I can't come something came up. I'll hit you up later."

"What came up? Let me guess ole girl and her daughter, you are so disrespectful. We couldn't even enjoy each other because you couldn't keep your eyes off her. You told me that you weren't seeing anyone."

"Look Miasha I'm not about to argue with you. For two reasons it's cold as fuck and, me and you ain't got shit going on. Yeah, I wanted to fuck after this, but some shit came up, and I'll have to keep my dick in my pants, and I'll get up with you another time.

Don't call me I'll call you." She wanted to argue. I'm not about to do that shit. If you already know what it is why ask. I circled the parking lot to see if I could see what Giselle was driving and her Porsche truck stood out.

I pulled up on the side of her truck on the passenger side. It was cold as shit out here. I had the heat blasting. I placed my hands on my head waiting on Giselle's fine ass to come out. She finally came strutting out I waited for her to put her daughter in the car before I approached her. I walked up behind her and tapped her on the shoulder.

"Giselle, can I speak to you for a minute?" She jumped.

"Yeah give me a minute. Are you stalking me?" She hit the push to start button on her truck.

"Get in for a minute. I don't want you standing out here in the cold." She got in, and I just looked at her.

"What's up?"

"You."

"Make it quick Dro because my truck will shut off in ten minutes and I can't have my daughter out in the cold."

"Why did you stop responding when I would text and call you? Did you meet someone else? I thought we were good. You just cut a nigga off."

"Look, Dro, I didn't meet anybody like you did. I'm going through some shit, and it's not fair, to make you wait on me, while I get through what I'm going through. It has nothing to do with you, but everything to do with me."

"You got me feeling some type of way. Did you get my text? I told you it wasn't anything. If it was, I wouldn't be here. It's something about you that has me gone; you put a spell on a nigga. Are you worth the wait? Can I help you get through what you're going through? You don't have to be alone. I told you day one that I got you and my word is law."

"Yes, and yes."

"What does that mean baby be specific?"

"Yes, Dro you can help me. You know I'm worth it."

"When I call you answer your fucking phone. I have connections, and I'll pull up on your ass if another call or text goes unanswered. I want you to try me, so you can see, how serious I am."

I grabbed her by the face and forced my tongue down her throat she knows that she's feeling the kid.

"Why did you do all of that?"

"You didn't stop me either."

"I don't know where your lips have been."

"If you stop playing games, you wouldn't have to worry. I only want my lips on you." Giselle knows what it is. I walked her to her truck and closed the door and watched her pull off.

Giselle

He does the most I swear. I knew that was him parked next to me. I didn't even look that way because I knew he was sneaky. I couldn't stop smiling he was so aggressive it doesn't make any sense. I loved everything about him, his caramel complexion fury eyebrows. He had a perfect set of lips and his teeth were white. Thank God Kassence nosey self was asleep because she would ask me a million questions about what Mr. Dro and I were talking about.

***

I made it home in thirty minutes top. I had to carry Kassence to her room and put her pajamas on. I left my purse in the car. I ran back out to get it. I had a three missed Facetimes from Dro. I jumped in the shower quickly to handle my hygiene, and I'll call him back when I get finished. I handled my hygiene and put my night clothes on. I sent Dro a text and asked him what's up.

He hit the Facetime button again. I answered. He was driving.

"You're hard headed. I'm on my way over there."

"And I hit you back. I had to put my daughter to bed and take a shower. I shot you a text. Give me some credit."

"I didn't text you though. I hit the Facetime button because a nigga wanted to see you, so that doesn't count. I'll be there in about twenty minutes."

"Whatever." He's crazy he just wanted to come over here anyway. Who was I to stop him, but he couldn't spend the night. I didn't want him around Kassence if he wasn't going to be permanent in my life. I needed to speak with Momma Edith, it was too expensive to call her, so I always used Facetime. I hit the connect button she answered on the first ring.

"Hey, my child what are you doing up this late? How was dinner you look better and sound better from when we spoke earlier?"

"It was great. I ran into someone."

"Who?"

"Momma, why do you sound like that? You're so funny acting, it was Dro."

"Stop playing with me you're hard headed. You're not about to get my blood pressure high. I told you that man was your husband, stop fighting it and let it flow. I know a few things, Giselle. I'm a prophet. I'll never steer you wrong. Blood doesn't make us family, but loyalty does."

"He was with someone?"

"And whose fault is that? I know you're going through some shit but get over it. You and Free have history and a shit load of memories. Let it go and create some new ones. Let Dro love you, how you should be loved. I only want the best for you. You deserve it."

"Mine, but he's coming over he said that it's nothing. I'm working on myself I promise you I am."

"Good because if my granddaughter Facetimes me one more time and tells me, you're sitting in the dark crying. I'm catching a flight to dig in your ass."

"Momma she told you that?"

"Yes, get out of your feelings and move on. Free isn't coming back live your life and be happy. She sees more than you think she does, she's very smart."

"I see."

"Enjoy yourself my child and call me in the morning to let me know if Dro took care of that ache that you have between your legs."

"Mother it's not that type of party."

"Bye my child," I swear Momma Edith has no filter, but she's always here when I need her for anything. Dro is crazy I'm not sure if he's coming or not but we'll see he thinks he's running things. Not.

Chapter-2

<u>Dro</u>

Giselle thought I was playing with her, but I'm not I can show her better than tell her. It's been about a month since I last saw her. Imagine how I felt when Kassence spoke to me. I can't believe she remembered me. A nigga was hoping and praying that the two of them didn't see me. Yeah, I was up to no good, but it's her fucking fault for cutting me off. I told her before we left each other when I call to answer the phone.

I called three times, and she didn't answer. She finally sent a text back asking what's up. I didn't send her a text. I wanted to see her via Facetime. I knew where she lived I wanted to pull up on her ass a few times. Tonight, was the night I'm sick of the little games that she's playing. I know she's been through some shit, but I'm not out to hurt her. I had a spot that wasn't too far from her house it'll take me about thirty minutes.

**

I pulled up at Giselle's house it was a little after 12:00 am. I threw my car into park and hopped out. Instead of ringing her doorbell because I had respect for her daughter I hit the Facetime button. She answered.

"Open the door."

"Dro are you really outside?"

"Open the fucking door and see. Are you going to leave a nigga out in the cold? Let me in." I hung up on her. She came and opened the door. I pushed her ass inside and backed her up into the corner. I grabbed her face and made her look at me.

"Dro."

"Giselle stop playing with me." I pulled her to the sofa that sat in the living room. She sat beside me and looked at me.

"What I do?"

"You don't know?" I had to enlighten her on what she had done.

"I'm sorry."

"Yeah, you better be."

"I'm serious."

"How you been?"

"To be honest Dro I've been going through a lot since I've been back. I thought I could deal with everything that happened, but it's been a task within itself. I'm okay now. I just prayed about it, and hopefully this will pass too like everything else." She turned her back to me when she spoke. I lifted her body up and sat her on my lap.

"Look at me when you are talking, don't ever do that. Let me in I swear I want to be here for you. I can't do that if you're shutting a nigga out. I promise you I'm not like them, other niggas. I'm in a league of my own."

"You have a funny way of showing it. Who was ole girl?"

"Nobody, I just took her to dinner. We were going to Netflix and Chill, but I see something better that caught my eye and attention. You mad?"

"You want me to be honest? Yes, I was a little salty, you knew that. You left a good impression on me. I'm feeling you."

"Good, why do you keep fighting it?"

"Who is that blowing up your phone?"

"Here answer it."

"Hello."

"Can I speak to Dro?"

"He's tied up with me right now, do me a favor and lose his number." Giselle laid down the law with Miasha. I don't have shit to hide. How can she be telling a female to lose my number if she's playing games and shit?

"You know you mine, right?"

"Dro, you can't stake claim to me, and you haven't officially asked me out."

"I'm a grown ass man. I do what the fuck I want, and not what I can. Baby, you know what it is."

"You're not playing fair."

"It's my world. I make my own fucking rules. I do what I want when I want. The moment you sat in my passenger seat in one of my foreign whips I felt the chemistry. You and I were already written let's make history. I'm a boss, and I'm about to take you on the wildest ride of your life."

"I'm scared."

"Don't Be. I wanted to see you for a little while. I'm about to bounce can I see you tomorrow?"

"Yes." I gave Giselle a peck on the lips. She walked me to the door. It was going on 3:00 am. I had to get to home and get me some sleep. A nigga was tired I've been running these streets since 8:00 am. It's time for me to lay it down. In all my years of living settling down with a female wasn't something that I wanted.

Why because I live a dangerous ass life. I've been in streets for a long time since a nigga was seventeen. I even got a few felonies in the process, but it's time for a nigga to change some shit up. Now was the perfect time to leave this shit alone. I have two sons that I want to see grow up. Unlike my father he watched me grow up from behind bars. I don't want that for myself.

I don't know if I could leave the streets alone because that's all I know. I've put my blood sweat and tears in this shit for years. I want to change so badly, but that shit is easier said than done. Whenever I think about changing and letting this shit go, something pulls me back in. I need too. It'll make my mother proud.

I've been out here running wild for a very long time, with no thoughts of easing up.

Chapter-3

<u>Giselle</u>

"Mommy wake up. I'm going to be late for school."

"I'm getting up Kassence; your clothes are already laid out."

My alarm has been going off for a minute. I hit the buzzer a few times. I'm tired Dro left a little after 2:45 am. He called me when he made it home, and we talked on the phone with each other for a few minutes.

I had to force myself to sleep I couldn't stop thinking about him. When sleep finally consumed me, it was time to take Kassence to school. What am I supposed to do, with him coming on so strong? I didn't agree to be in a relationship with him; he just forced me. I didn't have a choice. The funny thing about this whole situation it feels right nothing feels wrong about it. I'm not second guessing it.

It's a little after 8:00 am, I dropped Kassence off at school. I didn't have class today. Majority of Free's stuff was packed up and ready to be taken to the basement.

The contractors were scheduled to come by tomorrow to give me an estimate on everything that I wanted to be done. I needed to go to grocery store. Kassence wanted some white chicken chili. Of course, I was going to make my baby some. My phone started ringing it was Dro on Facetime.

"Good morning."

"Good morning, shouldn't you be sleeping?"

"Nope, my body is adjusted to getting up early. What are you about to do?"

"Finish packing up a few things and run a few errands later."

"Have you eaten?"

"No."

"Let me feed you. I'm going to shoot you my address I want you to pull up."

"Okay." I was not ready to see him just yet. I wanted to think about him for a few hours. I typed his address in on my phone. He didn't stay far from here. I couldn't wear what I had on now. I had to change clothes. Fuck it; he can see the real me.

He knows that I clean up nice when I do clean up. I'm hungry too I don't look that bad.

<u>Dro</u>

A few hours of sleep were all I needed. I had to get back to this money and most of all I wanted to see Giselle before I started my day off. I knew she wasn't expecting me to hit her up so soon. I'm serious as fuck about wanting to start something with her. I know I came off stand offish but so fucking what. She was single, and it wasn't about to be any niggas in line, but me.

My mother taught me how to cook everything. She didn't see me settling down any time soon, so she made sure a nigga knew how to cook. I understood it. I was whipping Giselle and me up something. Fish, grits, scrambled eggs with cheese and some French toast. It only takes her thirty minutes to get here she should be pulling up soon.

***

Giselle finally brought her ass over she was running late. Instead of her calling to let me know she was outside she rung my doorbell a few times. She better be glad I'm not a petty ass nigga, or I would make her wait a few minutes. I had my apron on I had to wash my hands before I opened the door. I swung the door open, and she looked at me with the biggest smile on her face.

"I don't know why you're smiling you late as fuck and who told you to change?"

"I'm not that late Dro; I had to change my shirt. It was my night shirt."

"Yeah, whatever. I know how you look. I didn't get at you because of your looks that's just a bonus. I like that real you, no make-up, no lip stick, no weave. If your natural hair was nappy as fuck, it wouldn't matter. I'll help you put a good pressing comb through it. I'm a sucker for you in those fitted jeans."

"Whatever Dro. I see you got jokes today. Why didn't you tell me that you stayed close by? Are you going to be a gentleman and show me around? It took you long enough to answer the door. It smells good in here, what are we eating?"

"Damn nosey let me get to that. I had to make sure my old lady was gone before my new one pulled up. I don't live here I just crash here when I'm in this area. I'll show you around come on."

"Dro don't start playing with me. If that's the case, I could've told my old nigga he could stay, and I'll see my new nigga another day."

"What you say?"

"You heard me." I jacked Giselle up and threw her on my couch. I climbed on top of her. I grabbed her face, so she could look at me. I'm a crazy wild ass nigga, and I don't play games.

"Don't play with me this shit ain't no game. I'm going to show you; how real this shit gets. Take me to your old nigga, so I can ask him, did he have plans to see you before I did. I told you what it was last night. Give me your damn phone?" I snatched her phone out of her hand; she had the new iPhone X that your face unlocks your phone. If she had any niggas number in her phone, I was deleting that shit.

"Damn you sexy as fuck when you mad, and aggressive. Don't dish it if you can take it."

"Keep playing, you better be glad everything looks good in here, or it'll be some fucking problems." I gave Giselle the tour of my condo. She agreed to fix our plates. I'm glad she wasn't shy to eat in front of me. I caught her looking at me a few times while I was eating.

"This is really good."

"I know, my mother taught me a few things."

"Is this something that you do for all of your girlfriends?"

"Look don't assume shit. Just because you saw me with her at that restaurant don't mean shit. Did she want me to fuck her of course? Did I no. When she called my phone, I let you answer that motherfucka, so you could know, and she could know what time it is. I'm explaining myself, and this is some shit that I normally wouldn't do. I never had a girlfriend, besides you I've only cooked for one other person."

"What would make you think that I would want to be with someone, whose never been in a relationship?"

"The same you've been in relationships with motherfuckas who have. I haven't met a female who was worthy of my time, so shit I wasn't trying to be committed. Look don't compare me to them. Give me a fair shot. Don't look at me like that, shit you asked."

"I'm not judging you at all, never that I just can't believe you're so blunt about the situation."

"What you see is what you get with me. I'll never lie to you, and I'll never judge you no matter what. Ain't nobody perfect I damn sure don't want to be.

Everybody has flaws; some people just hide theirs well. I wear mine on my sleeve."

Chapter 4

<u>Giselle</u>

"If I fall, Dro, you better catch me?"

"Always." Dro and I have been dating for about a month now officially. Everything felt so natural with him. Kassence loved him. We haven't crossed that line yet. I was more than ready to explore him. I'm nervous I must admit. I met his two sons a few weeks ago; he wanted me to meet his mom. I was a little nervous about that. Free's mother Farrah our relationship was decent. Now Juelz mother that was a different story.

Dro assured me that his mom was cool. Let me be the judge of that. I haven't heard from Journee in a few days. Jueleez spent the night last weekend with Kassence. Juelz dropped her off it was awkward. He threw his hand up. Dro was standing behind me in the door with his arms wrapped around my waist. I never got the chance to formally apologize to Juelz, but I will soon. I'm turning a new leaf and trying to right my wrongs.

"Baby what's on your mind? Talk to me."

"A lot Dro, but I don't want to bother you with my problems."

"Giselle, if we're going to be together, then your problems are my problems. Communication is the key. If we don't have that we won't have anything, as your man, I take on everything that comes with you."

"Dro, you're so perfect, what did I do to deserve you?"

"Giselle, you're perfect and more than worth it. You deserve me, why not you?" I swear Dro is something serious. He's a different breed. I'm not trying to fall for this man so soon, but damn he's making it real hard for me.

"Tell me what's on your mind, Giselle. I'm listening carefully." Dro picked me up and laid me on his chest and stroked the side of my face. He was sweet and gentle with me. No man has ever handled me the way Dro handled me. Underneath the gentleman was a boss and a savage. Of course, I asked around about him, and I was intrigued with what I heard.

"I want to right my wrongs with Juelz and his family. It keeps tugging at me. Journee and I have moved passed our differences.

Juelz and I haven't discussed ours."

"I got you Giselle, but let that shit go. If it was an issue do you think that he would agree to let his daughter come over? Two wrongs don't make a right. He has what he wants, and I have what I want. You don't have to explain yourself to anyone. You've done enough of that."

"Thank you."

"It's getting late, let me get up out of here."

"I want you to stay."

"Giselle, I would love to stay, but I don't want to shack up with you. I have plans for us and shacking up isn't a part of the process."

"If you say so, I'll miss you." I walked Dro to the door, and he kissed me on my lips. I didn't kiss him back. Yep, I was in my feelings.

"Giselle, don't do that. You don't know how bad a nigga wants to stay with you. Trust me I do. I'm changing my ways for you be patient with a nigga. In due time, it won't be any lonely nights."

"Okay." I have trust issues, and he knows that. I'll be patient for now. I pray Dro is different than the rest.

Lord knows I can't deal with another fuck nigga. I slid down the crack of the door and rested my head up against the door and closed my eyes.

I don't know how long I can keep going on like this. I'm trying to be patient and go with the flow, but if he's not sleeping with me is he sleeping with someone else? I knew Free had someone else and I was content with that because I had Juelz.

Juelz only slipped up a few times throughout our relationship. Being with Dro feels different than anything I've ever felt before. I've been hurt twice, and I would hope and pray that God wouldn't take me through anything close to what I've already endured.

Part of me moving on, I must let go of the past to have a better future. I don't want to ruin the chances of me being happy.

"Mommy, what's wrong?"

"Nothing Kassence, why do you say that?"

"You're sitting by the door instead of coming up to bed."

"I was just thinking about something's, and this was the perfect place." Kassence is on me like white on rice. She knows what's up. I got up off the floor and grabbed Kassence hand and walked up to my room. She climbed inside of my bed with me and laid on my chest. My big baby is so precious, my phone alerted me that I had a text it was from Dro.

Him- Get your ass off the floor, be patient with me. Trust me I don't want to sleep alone.

I couldn't do anything but smile. One thing about Dro, he kept a smile on my face. I didn't even know I had dimples until I started fooling with him, he brought those out.

Dro

Kassence sent me a text stating that her mother, was upset that I left. I had to pull over and shoot a quick text. I love Giselle I really do, the moment I laid eyes on her. I had to make her mine. I'm not a perfect nigga, but I'm a changed nigga. I haven't cuffed many broads.

Chanelle, she's the mother of my two sons we just happened. That was it, she caught feelings, but we didn't work out for more reasons that one. Kaniya was the closest thing I had to cuffing with any female I gave her a glimpse of my world.

We crossed paths at the wrong time, if I would've met her before Lucky than yes, we could've happened. I love my life, and I'm not trying to kill a nigga, behind no pussy that doesn't have my last name.

I never sampled it I just tasted it. Kaniya and I couldn't be together she was made for Lucky and Giselle was made for me. With Giselle, I'm different I wanted to change my ways. Fucking different broads Monday through Sunday. Making it rain in Magic on Monday. Making a mess in Onyx on Tuesday catching a flight on Friday fucking it up in KOD on Saturday. I didn't want to do that anymore. I think I could wife her. Giselle has trust issues.

I want to be the man that changes that, but she must let me in. I wanted more from her than sex. When I make love to Giselle, I want to make love to her mind body and soul. I swear I didn't want to leave her tonight, but I don't want to shack with her. I wanted to wife her, and she needed to understand that. I'm authentic not a fraud.

Her eyes were begging me to stay. I wanted to show her different. Trust me kicking it with her for three months and being committed is hard. I have blue balls every day fucking with her. I'm a boss ass nigga with savage tendencies and for her sake and not mine, she better glad I'm doing shit differently.

Chapter 5

<u>Kaniya</u>

"Mrs. Williams, we received another package from Foot Work, what do you want us to do with the packages?"

"Today is Thursday, and he should be open."

"We tried to take the packages there, and some female, told us to come back when he gets there, she wouldn't let us drop them off."

"Run that shit back Mya."

"She said that we couldn't leave the stuff."

"Follow me." I had to make sure I was hearing her correctly. Dro gets his stuff shipped here all the time. I need to nip it in the bud because Lucky doesn't want me housing shit here for any man that's not him. I can't do shit but respect that. It was the beginning of the winter, and I just had Jeremiah six weeks ago, I really shouldn't even be out.

Lucky didn't want me working. He wanted me to stay at home and be a housewife and work from home. I put my pea coat on and slid my foot in my heels and placed my gun behind my back. I don't know who this bitch was that worked at Dro's, but these packages had to get out of Work Now Atlanta. I marched down to his suite and opened the door.

It was a dark skin chick; her skin was so beautiful that shit glistened she grilled me. I smiled at the bitch. I walked back to Dro's office, and he was sitting there eating. I dropped the boxes on his desk Mya, and Kansas had the remaining boxes and dropped them also. The pretty girl, she was right on my heels too.

"Nice to see you to Kaniya."

"Dro, these packages, can't come to my office anymore. Please check your help and let her know, how this shit goes."

"Dro you better check this bitch and let her know what it is. I'm not the help."

"Excuse me, what the fuck did you just say to me?"

"You heard what the fuck I just said." My face turned candy red I flared my nose up. I had a blade in my jaw. I could slice this hoe the fuck up, or I could empty a clip in her. The choice was hers if she kept talking.

"Look Kaniya, don't come up in here with that bullshit. She ain't the help." Oh, so Dro is trying to show off and impress a bitch. Dro ain't even my nigga, and this bitch ain't my bitch. See the devil was on my back. I wasn't even about argue with Dro. I'll address his bitch first then him. I don't know who this hoe thought I was, but I'm one bitch that she needs to respect. I turned around Mya and Kansas were right on my heels. I stopped at the door right by ole girl.

I grabbed my gun from the nape of my back. I pointed it at her head first.

"You ain't my bitch, and you should never address me as one. I don't give a fuck if you're this niggas bitch. Call me a bitch again. You better ask your nigga how real this shit get. I don't mind bodying a bitch right here and right now. I don't tolerate disrespect at all."

"Kaniya chill out. Back the fuck up." Dro walked up behind me.

"Nah Dro I want this bitch to speak the fuck up. I stay at a hoe neck about my respect. If she got an issue, I'd solve it. I'm waiting." I put my index finger on the trigger ready to lay a bitch down.

"Kaniya, put the gun down. It's not that serious." I turned around and looked at Dro and grilled the fuck out of him. My gun was still pressed at the temple of ole girl's head.

"Nah Dro, it's serious for me because I didn't come down here on no fuck shit. My two employees brought your fucking shoes down here. Mya and Kansas, was this the bitch that said bring it back when Dro gets here?"

"Yes."

"That's not the way shit goes. They drop your packages off and keep it moving. Since it's a fucking problem find someone preferably your bitch to collect your shit when you're not open. Re-route that shit because Work Atlanta is no longer your drop off spot." I walked off and kept it moving. Fuck Dro and whoever this bitch was. I walked back to my suite.

"Mrs. Williams, you're bad that was dope as fuck."

"I like to show my ass every now and then because I can. It's not a bitch walking that can see me. I put that on everything." I smiled and walked back to my office. Dro knows better to disrespect me and talk to me like he's fucking crazy.

If Lucky knew I went down there and showed my ass, he would go off. I haven't seen Dro in almost a year since Lucky pulled up on us acting a fool.

"Mrs. Williams, you have company."

"I'm not expecting anyone." Dro busted in my office like he owned this motherfucker. I just looked at him and rolled my eyes. I had to cut the cameras off. I didn't need any problems with Lucky. My husband had this bitch wired, and Dro knew that. He slammed my door.

"Kaniya, you're wrong as fuck for doing that shit. You take shit too far. You didn't have to pull a gun out on my girl and press it on her head and attempt to pull the trigger. Lucky needs to give you some act right. A lady should never act the way you do."

"Are you finished? If so you can raise the fuck up out of here, the door is that way."

"No, I'm not leaving, you're going to listen to me."

"I'm not, the only man I listen too, is my husband and you ain't him. Goodbye Dro."

"You showed your ass because I got somebody? You're mad that I'm cuffing a female that's not you?

It's okay we all miss a good thing sometimes. I'm glad Lucky finally married you, he should've done it years ago.

I finally found somebody that's for me and no strings attached, no baggage and this is how you do shit? Since I met you, I've always been a good nigga to you, whatever you wanted I gave it to you. I've never disrespected Lucky behind you when I wanted too. I kept that shit savage. I had plenty of opportunities to put that nigga to sleep, but I didn't.

You know why because I didn't want to break your heart and see you cry because of some shit I did. I love Giselle, do you fucking hear me, and I will never let anybody disrespect her not even you. Yeah, I used to lust the fuck out you, but that shit doesn't matter anymore. You picked him and not me. I'm a real nigga, and I'm going to correct you when you're wrong."

"Dro you talk a really good game. It's not about you and her. Congratulations on your relationship I'm happy for you. You deserve it. I didn't mean to be disrespectful, but you know me. Not one time did you correct her and put her in her place.

I'm doing you a favor. Since you got that off your chest you can leave. Let me correct you it's only two motherfuckas that'll put Lucky to sleep and that's me and God." Dro wanted to say something else I put my hand up and pointed to the door. He's said enough.

Dro

Talking to Kaniya was pointless, she wasn't trying to hear shit I had to say. I could tell Giselle was pissed, by the look and scowl on her face was menacing. I walked back to my office, and Giselle was sitting behind my desk pissed off.

"I'm sorry."

"You should be. Why didn't you tell me the arrangement y'all had going on? Is this the type of shit that I need to look forward to fucking with a man like you? If so I'm out. I don't do females with guns."

"I honestly forgot, normally the packages are at the door waiting for me when I come in, the salesperson handles the stocking. Wait where are you going? I said I'm sorry, that will never happen again. You're ready to walk out on me that quick. You're supposed to have my back-like I have yours. Anything worth having ain't easy."

"I'll be back Dro I need to cool off," I swear if Giselle leaves me behind this shit. I'll fuck around and play God and murk Lucky just because Kaniya took shit too far. I see now this taking the high rode shit ain't for me.

I'm a boss in the sheets and a savage in the streets. Kaniya pulled Giselle's hoe card, and now she's tripping.

I should've told Giselle about the arrangement, but I didn't think that this shit would happen like this. Kaniya is so over the top with everything. They both were out of line. I should've corrected Giselle, but I didn't because she would've felt like I still had feelings for Kaniya. A nigga can't win for loosing. Kaniya was special to me. I can't pursue something that I can't have.

Giselle

It's not even 12:00 pm and shit is crazy. I had to cool off my blood pressure was high as fuck. I couldn't stop shaking. How did Dro think I was going to react when those two young thots came in here asking for him with some packages? How was I supposed to know those were shoes?

To make matters worse, the Kaniya chick strutted in here with her Pea coat and baby doll dress and walked straight back to Dro's office without asking any questions and smiled at me. I instantly thought that something was up. Who wouldn't, and her thots were following. Put yourself in my shoes.

I probably shouldn't have called her a bitch, but she was acting like one. She put the gun to my face so quick. I couldn't even tell she was carrying I've never experienced that before. I just knew this crazy bitch was going to pull the trigger. Y'all can call me crazy, but I felt the tension between her and Dro. I know he told me that it was nothing there, but I felt it. Let me call Journee. I dialed her number, she answered on the first ring.

"What's up Giselle?"

"Everything can you talk for a few minutes?"

"Sure, what's wrong?" I gave Journee the rundown of what happened she was speechless.

"Giselle, I'm going to keep it real with you. Can I do that?"

"Duh, that's why I called you."

"Dro is your man, and you have every right to speak your mind. You were wrong, and she was too. You shouldn't have called her a bitch first. She should've just spoke with you instead of walking in there like she ran shit. Pulling out a gun on somebody is a bit much. You and she should talk to clear the air since the two of you will be seeing each other to avoid any future problems."

"Journee why do you always say the right shit? I was wrong I can admit that, if you would've saw this bitch when she walked in. She had on this black baby doll dress that flared, and a pea coat, some fishnet tights, and Red bottoms. That's the come fuck me outfit. She was real pretty. Her hair was red and bone straight she gave me a nasty smirk. So, I popped off you know my mouth is foul. I'll talk to her."

I finished chopping it up with Journee. Dro sent me a few texts. I walked back to his store. I stood in the door just looking at him, he was so sexy.

"Oh, she does love me!" Dro walked up to me and slammed his office door. He pressed me up against the wall. He was all in my face. We were lip to lip. His cologne invaded my nostrils. I looked him in the eyes. Dro is the only man that I love to look in his eyes, for some reason. It's like I can see through him. His eyes tell me what he's feeling.

"Don't ever walk out on me again. I love you, and I mean it. You were wrong, and normally I would put you in your place, but as your man, I will never address you in front of anyone only in private." He bit my lips and slid his tongue into my mouth. He sunk his teeth into my neck, I started moaning because it felt so good.

"Apologize."

"I'm sorry Mr. Shannon." I moaned.

"You better be."

Dro and I exchanged passionate kisses. Damn, he was romantic. I was hot and bothered. I wrapped my legs around his waist. I told Dro that I had to pick up Kassence.

He said that he'd come by the house when he leaves. I had about three hours before Kassence was scheduled to get out of school. I had to go holla at Kaniya. I need to know what's up. I marched into her place of business the two thots were at the door.

"Welcome to Work Now Atlanta, may I help you?"

"Yes, I'm here to see Kaniya."

"Is she expecting you?"

"No, she's not."

"May I get your name?"

"Giselle." I sat and waited patiently. It was nice. She has nice taste. How can something so beautiful be so aggressive?"

"Giselle, she'll see you. Straight to the back on your right." I walked back to her office. Her door was closed. I knocked.

"Come in." I opened the door and looked around. We looked at each other."

"How can I help you?"

"We started off wrong." Her office phone rung and interrupted her; she put her hand up to take the call. It was on speaker phone. Oh, my God, the man on the other end was going in. The whole time she was smiling.

"Lucky, I have to go I have a guest, check the cameras you can see that right? I'm sorry my husband is crazy, and I can guarantee you he'll be here in about thirty minutes. So, whatever you need to say make it quick because he pissed."

"I'm sorry for calling you a bitch, but you were way out of line, and very disrespectful."

"I'm always out of line, and I'm a disrespectful ass bitch if provoked. You provoked me, and you know that. Dro was out of line too, but y'all can have that. He has packages that come here every day. Just make sure that somebody is at the store to sign for them. For the record, I, don't want Dro I'm happily married. My husband is it for me."

"I'm Giselle Lawrence and Dro, and I are dating. We've been dating for about three months now. He told me about you, but he didn't say that you were bat shit crazy, when you walked in the door. You gave me a seductive smirk. Look at how you're dressed that's a come fuck me outfit. You were rude; you walked straight back to his office without asking any questions. So yes, I played my position and my guard was all the way up."

"Congratulations Dro deserves it. I understand your position and I would do the same if not worse when it comes to my husband. I'm sorry my employees just told me that they couldn't drop off the packages. I couldn't have the stuff in the lobby. I'm not threat."

"Thank you! I'm sorry about that, but Dro didn't tell me about the arrangement that two of you had setup. Can I ask you a question?"

"Sure, depending on what it is." She wrote on a piece of paper that her husband is listening and watching does she need to cut the mics."

"No, I couldn't even tell that you were holding. I was shaking when you stood by me and pulled out and pressed the gun to my head. Can you teach me how to do that?"

"Giselle, you're going to get me fucked up? My husband is going to trip if he finds out I done that. You look like a good girl pretty, sweet and innocent I'll corrupt you if allowed."

"I'm sorry. You know the saying never judge a book by its cover. I would love to be corrupted."

"If you say so, take my number, I normally go to the gun range on Tuesdays. You can come with me if you like. Ask Dro he may not want you in the mix with me." Kaniya was nice, but she didn't apologize for shit. The way that she talks about her husband I hope to talk about Dro like that one-day.

I hopped in my Porsche and pulled off. I left my phone in the truck. Dro sent me a text asking me where I was and why did I lie about going to pick Kassence up. I turned around and went back to his office to speak with him.

Dro and I didn't have any secrets between us. I had to speak with this Kaniya chick I'm good at reading people and she didn't have any interest in Dro.

"Don't start lying to me, Giselle."

"I didn't lie I'm headed there now. I had to speak with Kaniya last; I checked you didn't have a gun pointed at your head. Everything is cool now, but I'll see you later okay."

I attempted to walk off from Dro, and he grabbed me and gave me a hug, I swear everything feels so right with him.

Chapter-6

<u>Lucky</u>

My wife has tried me for the last fucking time. I love Kaniya I swear to God I do, but I will fucking hurt her, and she doesn't believe that shit. I don't ask for much but pussy on demand, respect, and loyalty that's it. Our love is unconditional, and we have a bond that can't be broken. She takes advantage of that shit.

I know I'm not perfect and I've done some foul ass shit to her. A lot of people think that we shouldn't be together, and I don't deserve her. I don't give a fuck what they think. The things that we went through has brought us here today. I watch my wife's back like I watch my own. Any move that she makes I can account for it. Any conversation that she has I'm listening.

I didn't want Kaniya working at all. We have three small children, Jamel, Jamia, Jeremiah. I want a fourth one.

My youngest son just turned six weeks old. Jamia and Jamel just turned one. Kaniya needs to be at home with them period. Kaniya can run Work Now Atlanta from home; she acts like she couldn't stay in the house.

Today was her first day back. I left the house early this morning. I had some business to handle with my brother Quan. I came back home and checked the cameras because I didn't see her when she left. She looked nice she was complaining about her weight because of Jeremiah. I told her she was fine and that she was.

My wife brings out the best in me and the worst. I was sitting back in my office at home, and the camera feed to Kaniya's office was killed. I had back up and brought it back up. I hit rewind to see what happened and why. Dro walks in, that's the first red flag. I know that's why she killed the camera. I heard the exchange between the two of them.

Am I mad at my wife, yes, the fuck I am. It's not about because she killed the cameras. I trust Kaniya I trust her with my life. I let Kaniya get away with a lot of shit. She had no business going into Dro's period. I told her month's ago, to stop signing for shit for him. Did she listen no.

I'm pissed because Dro handled my wife like he was me. I'm the only man that can handle my wife and check her about anything. Her father can't even do it. Dro was a funny ass nigga, whoever this bitch was that he was fucking with she had him feeling himself.

He said he could've put me to sleep. I rubbed my hands across my face I know this nigga didn't say this shit. Every nigga that I've got at behind my wife I left them still breathing for a reason. It's always a method to my madness. If they could get at me as I've got at them, then we can shoot it out that out fair and I'll still win. I'm bulletproof it's cocky to say, but I AM.

If Dro had an issue with me, it was never addressed. I'll step on anybody's toes behind my wife. Dro was just something for Kaniya to do, she knew better than to cross that line with him. She only fucked with him to get under my skin, and that shit worked too.

Kaniya she'll learn the hard way, she takes my kindness for my weakness, but I'll show her as her husband to never go against my fucking word and what I say do. Watch how this shit unfolds, she's expecting me to come and show out, but I'm not.

I'll get at Dro never speak on me and mention what you'll do to me, if you haven't done it. Don't ever disrespect my wife.

Dro

Today was crazy as fuck. I locked up the store and headed to my mother's house. I saw Kaniya walking to her car in the parking lot. We locked eyes with each other. Fuck Kaniya, a nigga like me isn't pressed with her and the shit that comes with her. I had to go holla at my OG, so she can help me make some sense with shit.

My mother stayed on the Southside I brought her house in Eagles Landing. I told her I was coming through. She said I haven't been through to see here since I've been with Giselle. I stopped by the flower shop to get my mother some roses. I used my key get in.

"Roderick get your ass in here now. When am, I going to meet Ms. Giselle? Kaniya called me and told me you showed your ass behind her today. It must be serious, but I still haven't met the heifer."

"Ma, what are you doing still talking to Kaniya?" Ugh, what was she still doing talking to her? I'm not surprised my mother loved Kaniya like she was hers.

"Look Dro or should I call you Roderick? Who I converse with is my business. I love Kaniya that'll never change no matter what.

We talk every day and do lunch once a month. I checked her about her shit, and I'm going to check you too."

"For what Ma, I didn't do anything wrong. She was out of line."

"You were too, understand that shit. You should've taken the packages and shut the fuck up. Last, I checked Kaniya was doing your lazy ass a favor, not the other way around. She shouldn't have pulled a gun out on the girl, I checked her please believe me I did. She did it to fuck with you."

"Look ma stop taking up for her."

"Whatever Roderick, give me my damn flowers, I'm not taking up for nobody. I'm just speaking facts. It's a crime for me to correct you when you're wrong, what did you come by for? I will never stop talking to Kaniya.

If you felt that way about her, you should've never introduced me to her. The next bitch you bring make sure it's your wife. I'm not in the business of being friendly with bitches you date okay. Do I make myself clear Roderick Shannon?"

"It's understood Ma." My OG just went straight in on me. I didn't know that Kaniya and my mother still had a relationship. I finished eating my liver and onions, cabbage and cornbread. My mother just grilled the fuck out of me and slapped the back of my head. I had to leave I promised Giselle that I'd come by there tonight. I kissed my mother on her cheek and told her I would see her in a few days.

My whole mood changed. Something didn't feel right. I patted my coat pocket to make sure I had my Glock on me. I checked my hip to make sure I had my .9mm on me. It was the beginning of winter, and it's hunting season. Everybody is trying to come to up. I used to be a jack boy. I know how this shit goes. I put a few niggas to sleep to get what I wanted.

When it is your time, it's your time. I could smell death in the air. I hope that motherfucka don't come my way. The moment you find happiness bullshit has a way to fuck it up. If I die today, let me call Giselle and tell her that I love her in case I don't see her again. I dialed her number.

"Hey baby, are you on your way?"

"I am I love you, and I'll see you in a few."

"I love you too Dro, hurry up I miss you."

"I'm trying. If I don't make it home, just know I love you."

"Baby, what are you telling me?"

"I love you, Giselle; I'll keep that shit one hundred with you. I'd never to lie to you. I've done a lot of shit in my life. I'm not the type of nigga that brags about nothing. What you see is what you get with me. Life ain't promised to nobody.

I've got a lot of bodies on my hand, more than I can count. I smell death in the air. It might be my time. I just want you to know that I love you and these last few months that we've spent together have been the best. I wouldn't trade any of it."

"Dro don't talk like that. Where are, you I'm coming to you?"

"I'm leaving my mother's house."

"Give me the address." she cried.

"Giselle, calm down baby. Don't cry just know I'll always make it home to you if I can. I'm good, just know when I go I'm not going down without a fight, if I can take a nigga with me trust me I will.

If a nigga thinks he can kill me and not die the same hand that he's dealing me. He has life fucked up."

"Dro do what you have to do to make it home to me. I can't be calm and stop crying because I'm falling for you and my heart is in this. I didn't want to give my heart to a boss ass nigga like you, but the moment you laid eyes on me you stole that shit from me. I'm at the door waiting and when you come. I'm not letting you go I hear what you are saying about that shacking up stuff. We have to figure something out."

"I hear you baby, we'll see, let me get off this phone, so I can make it to you." I'm feeling Giselle, and I haven't even sampled the pussy, not even put my mouth on it that's a first for me. I wanted to try something different with her. I'm an aggressive ass nigga, and I get anything I want. I wanted to charm her a unique way.

Giselle

Dro hasn't come home yet. I've called his phone at least twenty times. It's been over two hours. I think something happened to him. I can feel it something isn't right. I didn't want to keep calling Journee with my problems. I had to call somebody to calm my nerves; something told me to call Kaniya I don't know why but I did. I dialed her number, she answered on the first ring.

"Hello."

"Hi Kaniya, is this you?"

"Who wants to know?"

"This is Giselle, Dro's fiancé."

"What's up?"

"Can you talk?"

"Yeah, I answered the phone, didn't I?"

"Dro called me earlier telling me that he loves me, and how it feels like death is in the air. If he doesn't make it home, he wanted me to know that he loves me. He hasn't made it home; I feel like something is wrong. He was leaving his mother's house."

"Call Rodica."

"I don't know that lady."

"Hold on."

Okay."

"Ma, Dro over there?"

"Why Kaniya? Keep me out of you and Dro's shit. I already had to check you and him on the same day. Where is your husband, that's who you need to be fucking asking about?"

"Look Ma I ain't looking for him. Giselle is on the phone looking for her fiancé."

"Oh, excuse me, Giselle, that's how I have to talk to this heifer here. He's gone he left about two hours ago, I'm sorry Kaniya forgive me please."

"Nope, I ain't doing it. I had enough of you for today. Give Giselle your number so she can call you when she's looking for him okay." Mrs. Rodica gave me her phone number.

"Kaniya, I'm sorry I didn't mean to get you cussed out. It doesn't feel right; he would not answer unless something is wrong."

"I'm used to it now. Just pray on it. Maybe his phone is dead. I'm sure he'll make it home to you within an hour. If he doesn't call Rodica, she has access to his OnStar information she'll be able to track his car for you.

"Okay, that's cool." Dro's mother is off the hook. I swear the feelings that I have for Dro, it's unexplainable. It's like something that I never felt before. I'm emotionally attached to him. I feel it in my heart that something is wrong.

Out of all the men that I ever been with. I don't want to lose Dro. When I'm in his arms, I feel so safe and secure. I've never prayed for a man before, but I want to pray for Dro and do a lot of things different with him. I prefer to be safe than sorry. I called Dro's mother I wanted her to check his OnStar for me.

"Hello."

"Hi Mrs. Shannon, this is Giselle, Dro's girlfriend. How are you?"

"I'm good, how are you? Wait a minute I thought you were his fiancé?"

"I'm ok I'm worried about Dro that's why I called. He still hasn't made it home yet. I want to be his fiancé. I love the way it sounds. It sounds good, doesn't it?"

"Okay, Ms. Giselle I hear you. It does sound good. I've never met a female that has already put it out there, that she's my son's fiancé. So Dro's home is with you?"

"I'm glad to be the first. I want it to be."

"Let me check Dro's OnStar for you to see if I can get a location on him."

"Okay."

"Giselle, Dro's car is moving he's headed toward 85N at the Spaghetti Junction ramp."

"Okay, he's headed in my direction."

"Giselle, I want to meet you, when can we meet and have lunch? I hear it in your voice that you're sincere about my son and it moves me."

"What are you doing tomorrow?"

"Nothing."

"I have class, and I get out at 12:00 pick a restaurant, and I'll meet you there."

"I'll see you tomorrow I look forward to meeting you." Mrs. Rodica seemed nice. I think I might like her off her conversation alone.

Chapter 7

<u>Dro</u>

Man, it's raining like a motherfucka. Giselle is going to kill me. I've been stuck in traffic for almost two hours. It was a wreck, and I was behind that shit. My phone is dead, and this car charger isn't working. I should've gone home, because it's getting too late. I had no plans of staying the night with her. We're not ready for that yet. I'm trying to handle her different.

I promised her I would come by, and I didn't want to break my promise. Giselle had trust issues, and I wanted her to trust me. I pulled up in Giselle's driveway; the living room light was on. I hopped out of my truck and ran toward the porch and rang the doorbell. She swung the door open.

"You had me worried me." She took my coat and placed it on the ottoman and jumped on me. I wrapped my arms around her waist cuffed her ass and bit the nape of her neck.

"I see, you missed me." I carried her up to her room, and gently placed her on the bed and hovered over her, stuck my tongue down her throat. I loved the way the mint tasted on her breath. She was breathing heavy.

"I have a date tomorrow."

"You have a date, you want me to a kill a nigga, what the fuck are you trying to do Giselle?"

"Nothing Dro. Your mother and I are going to lunch. Is that okay with you?" She laughed and gave me a devilish smile.

"You talked to my mother?"

"Yes."

"How?"

"I called Kaniya because I was worried, and she told me to call your mother, and I didn't want to do it because I haven't officially met her, but I'm glad I did she's really nice and was very welcoming."

"Why would you call Kaniya? Don't get mixed up with her she's crazy."

"I like Kaniya despite our little run in earlier she's pretty cool and if I didn't call her my nerves would've been shot."

"I hear you."

"Are you mad at me?"

"No Giselle, I could never be mad at you. I'm glad my mother got the chance to speak with you. Now my two favorite ladies can meet, and take Kassence with you, so she can meet my princess."

"I'm your favorite?"

"Yes, and you can be more than that if you play your cards right. Trust me I got you."

"I trust you, Dro."

"Act like it."

"I do, more than you'll ever know."

"I have to get up out of here and get home. I don't break promises." Giselle tugged my shirt, and wrapped her legs around my waist, and gave me her bedroom eyes and pouted her lips.

"Nope, you're not leaving me tonight. You already scared me and had me worried that something was going to happen to you. Just the thought of not seeing you again had me in my feelings. I understand that you don't want to shack with me. I'm okay with that. I'll sleep better, and not stress if your here lying next to me. I want you to hold me."

"Look I'm not trying to stress you. I should keep it real with you Giselle, being in the streets death is a part of the game. We all must go someday. Thank God I dodged a bullet today." I'll lay here with you until you tap out, and then I'm going home."

"No Dro you're not going home tonight. I understand that you want to do a lot of stuff different with me and I'm open to that. Regardless I still want Dro the old and the new. You're my man, I want you to hold me at night, and when the suns come up, I want to turn over and still be wrapped in your arms.

I want to see you lying next to me. I want to handle your morning wood. I want to get a whiff of your morning breath. I want to cook you a good breakfast and see you off to work. I want you out of the streets and part of us being together we need to build together. We both can make changes together. You want to do stuff different with me, start by letting the street stuff go and bringing your ass home every night to me."

"Damn baby you got my third leg hard as fuck with that. You feel him? I need to put you on edge more often. I'm listening trust me I am. I'll see what I can do."

"Do it."

"I am."

"Good, go take a shower. It's some pajamas in the top right drawer."

"I'm not wearing Free's shit."

"Really Dro, you're too big to wear anything of Free's. I packed up Free's stuff months ago; I brought you some stuff in case you decided to stay the night with me, move get out, you can go home." I had Giselle pinned underneath me taking in all her sexiness. She was beautiful. I don't know what the fuck she's doing to me, but whatever it is I don't want her to stop.

"Baby you mad? You know me sleeping and holding you every night, will get you in a lot of trouble." Giselle had on these lace boy shorts I wanted to snatch right off her. I wanted to slide them down her thick chocolate thighs and dive in head first.

Her pussy was so hot I could feel it when she wrapped her legs around me.

I need to put that flame out. I started to eat her just for the fuck of it. I'm a savage and a beast in the sheets. She'll see.

Chapter 8

<u>Kaniya</u>

Lucky thinks he's slick. He should've been home by now. I called his phone at least ten times, to see where he's at. He said enough earlier, and I didn't feel like arguing. The same way he tracks me, I can track him.

I knew my husband better than I know myself. Any other time he would've pulled up, when I cut the cameras off. I wasn't trying to be sneaky. I just know him. He's cocky and he does the most. I can bet you any amount of money he's done something to Dro. I hope he didn't kill him. Dro was a good nigga and he didn't need to die behind me.

Giselle is really feeling him. He's a great guy I just couldn't be with him. I hope Lucky hasn't done anything crazy. My father agreed to come over and watch the kids. I tracked Lucky's phone; it was at a spot not too far from his club. I called his phone again to see if he would answer, and he didn't. Since when, did he think it was okay to stop answering the phone for me? My doorbell rang. I checked the cameras. It was my father.

"Kaniya, where are you going this time of night and where's Lucky?"

"Daddy I'm going to go find Lucky."

"Where the fuck is he?"

"Doing something he has no business doing."

"Look Kaniya; I'm not babysitting for you to go out and kill somebody behind him. Keep your ass at home with my grandchildren. He'll be home trust me."

"Ok daddy." My daddy kissed me on my forehead and left right out the door. He knew I was up to some good bullshit.

Lucky

Kaniya has been blowing up my phone up. I never ignore her, because she has my kids. I know she's tracked my phone, and she probably thinks that I'm out doing some dog ass shit, but I'm not. She's it for me I swear to God she is. A nigga is in his feelings. I'm an aggressive ass nigga, and that shit turns her on. I'm not trying to turn her on.

I'm battling with myself on how to check my wife and put her in her fucking place. I've let her slide one too many times. First, it was Tariq, and now it's Dro. The thing about Kaniya is if we get into an argument, she doesn't give a fuck. She'll tell me that I can leave, or I can go at any time and she ain't going to miss me. If I leave her, trust me she'll miss me when I'm gone.

We're married how in the fuck are you not going to miss your husband? I swear I don't want to hurt her, but sometimes you'll hurt a person to teach them. What more can I do? I'll never put my hands on her. She doesn't listen, and I hate when she doesn't listen.

I'll leave her just to teach her. I own up to all my shit before I started cheating on Kaniya she wasn't like this at all.

It's my fault I woke up a beast that can't be put to sleep. Me leaving her could make us, it ain't no breaking us.

***

It was a little after 1:00 am. I checked the cameras before I came home. Kaniya was asleep. I made my way upstairs. My dinner was on the counter, waiting for me. She made my favorite. If I stopped and ate my food. I'll end up staying and I wouldn't leave. I finally made my way to our room.

"You finally decided to come home?" She jumped out the bed and was instantly in my face.

"Look Kaniya take your ass to bed. I'm not trying to argue with you. Don't wake my fucking kids up."

"Lucky I don't give a fuck about none of that shit you're spitting. Answer me where have you been?" I wasn't about to answer her. I grabbed my body duffle bag from our closet and started packing my stuff. She smacked the back of my head. I grabbed her hands.

"Kaniya, keep your hands to yourself. I need a break from you, so I'm leaving."

"Oh, you leaving me, whoever she is make sure she's worth it. Let me help you pack your shit. Leave an address so I can have you served. It's a wrap." This is what the fuck I'm talking about. She doesn't give a fuck. I stopped packing my shit to address her. I turned around and was all up in her face. I grabbed her face, so she can understand me. I wanted her to feel the heat dripping from me, she needs to feel my heartbeat.

"It's not about a BITCH. You're the only BITCH that I want. I need some space from you because you don't give a fuck about me and my feelings. I will hurt you physically. You don't listen to shit I have to say. You think I'm a fucking a joke."

"Lucky, you." I cut her off.

"Stop fucking talking to me, please and take your ass to fucking bed. I'll be by to see my kids and maybe you tomorrow."

"Jamel Williams, you're really leaving our kids and me?" She cried. I'm not even about to answer her. I swear I didn't even think Kaniya had tear ducts. Not one time did she say she was sorry. Her tears moved me, but not enough for me to stop what I was trying to do.

All I wanted her to do was apologize, but she had too much heart and pride to do that. I grabbed my plate and walked back to my truck. I pulled out of our garage and went to my apartment in the city. I looked up at our room window, the curtains were pulled back, and Kaniya was standing in the window looking at me.

Kaniya

Lucky left me okay. I wiped the tears from my eyes with the back of my hand. I'm not even mad that he's gone. I pleaded, no, I begged him not leave. He's walked out on me not once but twice. It will not be a third fucking time. He wanted to be in his feelings today and express himself. Keep being in your feelings, because when I'm in mine, it'll be an issue for you and not me.

If he wanted to separate that's fine with me, but I'm divorcing him. He walked out on our kids and me. It's all good though. I watched him pull away and leave. I was tired, but I'm packing up everything he owns and sending it to his mother's house.

He thinks that I don't know he still had his Condo in the city. He wanted to be a hoe; he can be one. I'm done, and he'll see real soon, how done I am. I don't want anything to do with him. I needed to vent, let me call Killany to see if she's awake. I'm sure the boys have her ass up.

"What Kaniya?"

"Killany, what you are doing?"

"Breastfeeding."

"Oh."

"What's wrong Kaniya?"

"Lucky left me."

"He what?"

"You heard me; I'm good though."

"What did you do?"

"Why do you think that I did something? I'm me Killany that's all I can be. I told you what happened earlier, Giselle and I squashed that shit. You know what I shouldn't have called you because you are always judging a bitch.

It's sad I can't even call the bitch that I shared the same womb with to comfort me. You never ride for me, the way I ride for you. Good night thanks for answering."

"See Kaniya this is not what the fuck we're about to do. If it ain't your way, it ain't no way. You can't guilt trip me. Don't you ever let it come out your mouth that I don't ride for you, how you ride for me. I ain't never judged you bitch.

I'm not gone pacify you, as our mother does. The months I spent in the FEDS woke a bitch up. I stay woke. Let me keep it real with you. Lucky didn't leave you just because, he ain't gone never leave you. You did something, what the fuck did you do?

Can you please change your ways Kaniya? Fight for your marriage the same way that nigga fights and wreak havoc behind you. I'm surprised he didn't leave you months ago, you were nursing Tariq back to health, behind his back like your husband didn't know. You are accepting packages at your shop for Dro like your husband didn't know. If he did what you did how would you feel? Do you see what you caused?"

"How do you know all of this?"

"My husband of course."

"Lucky talks to Yung like that?"

"Everyday."

"Look Killany; Lucky is in his feelings about a lot of shit. If he didn't do what he did to Tariq, that situation would've never happened. He should've taken the high road and left it alone. My sister and I sister don't even speak because of that shit.

I miss Raven so fucking much, and I want to see my niece, but I got too much pride, to even reach out. Dro, was there for me when Lucky wasn't, he was with me at doctor's appointments, and I was pregnant with Lucky's kids. If I ever need Dro, he'll be there, not that I need him too. Some relationships can't be severed, so me accepting packages for him is minor. He would never cross that line with me again.

Yirah lives with Lucky's momma, and he always over there. Do you see me tripping? No, and trust me that bitch is trying to throw pussy at him every chance she gets. Am I not supposed to have any feelings about that shit? His mammy will keep Jamal but won't even acknowledge my three or anything, but he's in his feelings.

When I said I do, I was done with games. I have three kids and he ain't one of them. If he left, let the nigga leave. I'm not running up behind him. Eight years is a long time to be with someone. Maybe it's time for us to go our separate ways. Trust me I'm okay with that. We can co-parent."

"Kaniya are you up to something? You sound real sincere and chill about the shit."

"I'm not Killany, I've been with Lucky for a very long time. I just want to be by myself and with my three. I need to get back to the old Kaniya. Lucky took that from me two years ago; he woke up a beast that can't be put to sleep. I need to find me again. I just want to be alone."

"I got your back no matter what. Take some time for yourself."

"I am I love you; I got to go Jeremiah just woke up." For the first time in a long time. I was tired. I love Lucky, but I love myself more. I'm glad that he's gone. I'm tired of the arguing and small fights and the shit that he accuses me of.

If I walked out on him I wouldn't have made it to the hallway. He would've shown his ass, and probably beat mine, believe or not. I'm not on no get back shit. Any other time I would be glad to show my ass and bag another nigga just to show him. I don't have to do all of that. He knows what it is. He's free to do him. It's over...

Chapter 9

<u>Giselle</u>

Dro finally caved in and stayed the night with me. I was happy; it was everything that I imagined it to be. I understood what Dro was trying to do, but I wanted to feel all of him physically. He was big, and I wanted to see what his dick could do.

I laid on his chest and traced his tattoos with my manicured nail. He kept gripping my ass and making it shake with his big hands. Dro was a freak I could tell. My breast and nipples are my sensitive spot. I get turned on immediately.

He sucked each one with so much passion I had to make him stop. He laughed, he knew what he was doing. I asked him had he ever been raped before. He thought that shit was so funny. I grabbed his dick and told him if he keeps playing with me I'm taking it.

I was so turned on, to say I was hot and bothered was an understatement. I swear when Dro and I cross that line. I'm fucking the shit out of him because he made me wait so long.

His dick was so big it touched the middle of his thigh; I can't wait Dro has the type of dick that'll make a bitch climb the walls. I was ready to do just that.

It was cool being with Dro just to lay up until the sun came up and not fuck. He's really a different type of guy. When I woke up, I was wrapped up in his arms. I didn't need any cover; his body was all the heat I needed. He smelled so good, I cooked him a nice breakfast. Fish, cheese grits, potatoes and onions and homemade biscuits.

I sat the breakfast tray right next to him, with a glass of orange juice. Dro is the only man that I ever cooked for. I never cooked for Juelz or Free the two of them wasn't worthy of getting the real Giselle. My mother, aunts, and grandmother were great cooks, so of course, I could cook. I didn't cook when I was younger, but every dish my mother and grandmother made. I could tell you how to make it and what to put in it.

Dro made my morning. I couldn't stop smiling. I took a hot shower, and he stood and watched me. I told him to get in. He just took a picture. I had to take my baby to school. Kassence really loved Dro. Free left me financially straight. Kassence would never need anything. I'm grateful for that.

The old me I would've blown through this money, but the new me I'm about to invest. I'm going to school for hair, of course, I'm considering getting my hair line together. I wanted to open a boutique also I love fashion.

"Mommy, I love Dro for you."

"I love him for me too. Why do you like him?"

"Because mommy, you're always smiling and you're happy. I love it when you're happy, and we get to do a lot of fun things that we've never done before."

"Kassence I'm happy for many reasons. Everything that we're doing I will continue to do if Dro is in the picture or not. You're my baby girl, and it's my job to make you happy and do fun stuff with you. From here on out that'll never stop."

"Thank you, mommy. I love you."

"I love you too." Kassence brought tears to my eyes. It's crazy my baby knew that I wasn't happy she could tell. It has nothing to do with Dro. I'm not stressing about Free or Juelz. I know I'm number one in Dro's life. I can say that with confidence. I don't have to beg him to do anything. Everything that he does for me he does it because he wants too. He pays every bill here, and guess what he doesn't even lay his head here. Tonight, was the first night.

I'm happy and content right now the way everything is going. Things are finally looking up for me.

Dro

Last night was a good night despite the drama earlier. This morning was even better. Giselle really catered to me. Temptation a motherfucka I almost gave in this morning and let her handle my morning wood. I can't wait to bless her with some dick. If I gave it to her now, she'd really be gone. When I give it to her, she'll be gone a unique way. The breakfast was good I'm full. I had to call my partner to see what's up with her. She answered on the first ring and didn't say anything.

"Are you going to say something or you're just going to hold the phone?"

"I'm listening."

"I'm sorry."

"I'm sorry too."

"You did entirely too much yesterday. I appreciate you for looking out last night, and you didn't have too."

"You're good it wasn't a problem. I like her for you, for some reason. She's pretty. She said I'm Dro's fiancé. Bitch please that nigga ain't marrying nobody. It's must be the dick."

"I love her I swear to God I do. I haven't fucked her yet. I want to make her my wife. When I marry her, I want you to give me away at my wedding."

"Whatever Dro."

"I'm serious Kaniya; you know you're my nigga if your head and ass don't get no bigger. I'm dead serious."

"Bye Dro."

"Wait we're talking, can you can talk?"

"Yes."

"Where's your husband?"

"He left me last night."

"Are you okay?"

"I'm good you know me, I take the good with the bad it is what it is."

"Are y'all getting a divorce? Y'all haven't even been married a year."

"I don't even want to talk about it. Let's talk about you and Giselle. How do you know that she's the one and why hasn't Rodica met her?"

"I just know Kaniya. It's different with her. You know me. I'm a fucking savage and a boss ass nigga. I don't want her to see that side of me, but she wants all of me the old and new Dro. I haven't even tasted the pussy or broke her off yet. She's been through a lot, and I don't want to take her through anything else. She's been dealt a bad hand, but she finessed the situation. I want her to meet my mother, but she's scared because of her history with her EX's mother."

"Damn I can't believe you're ready to settle down. I'm happy for you Dro; you deserve it. I'll come to your wedding, and even throw your bachelor party, but I'm not giving you away. You are pushing it with that shit."

"You know I got your back no matter what. Never forget that. No matter who I'm with, we'll always have a bond. If you ever need me, I'm one call away."

"I know Dro some shit can never be severed. I was telling Killany that last night. You were there for me when that pussy ass nigga wasn't. I'm forever grateful for that. I appreciate you more than you'll ever know. I'll still sign for your packages. Giselle better not fuck up. You know I don't mind bodying a bitch."

"Chill out with that shit. I appreciate you too. Keep your head up Kaniya. It gets greater later like you always told me. Let me tell you this before I hang up. I'm on the outside looking in, and I have never judged you, never will. Every time that nigga left, you took him back.

I don't know what happened and you don't have to tell me. Ain't shit easy with you. You're one of the strongest females I know, and that's what attracted me to you. You will never fold that could be good and bad."

"He said I don't listen and take his feelings into consideration."

"That may be true, when you pulled the gun out on Giselle and pointed to her head.

I was done with you because you didn't have to do that. You just wanted to show her, how bad you were. Tone it down a little bit Kaniya; you have more heart than niggas and Lucky maybe intimidated by that."

"I hear you."

"Are you listening though?"

"I am Dro."

"Alright, I'm holding you too that let me get up off this phone." Kaniya and I would always be the best friends no matter what. We may not see each other every day, but if I call her, she would answer and call right back. She was happy for me. I appreciate that.

Chapter 10

<u>Rodica</u>

Roderick and Giselle! I couldn't wait to meet this woman whose captured my son's heart. I knew she had to be special, when Dro speaks about her it's the same way his father used to speak about me.

His face lights up, and I don't think I ever saw him smile the way he does when he talks about her. It was a little after 12:00 pm. She was meeting me at Spondivits. I made it here early I knew she said, that she had class. I tried calling Kaniya this morning her stubborn ass didn't answer the phone. We talk every day that was my daughter regardless if her and my son didn't work out we were cool. I noticed the host walking a female and her daughter my way. That must be Giselle.

"Hi, Mrs. Shannon. I'm Giselle, and this is my daughter Kassence." She gave me a hug; she seemed like a nice girl. She was beautiful too. Her daughter was the cutest little girl.

"Nice to meet you too Dro's fiancé, tell me about yourself?"

"My name is Giselle Lawrence, and I'm born and raised in Atlanta. I'm from Jonesboro. I'm twenty-seven. Kassence is my only child. I'm a homebody, and I'm infatuated with your son."

"Okay hi, Kassence. How old are you?"

"7 I'll be 8 in April."

"What are you going to school for, do you work?"

"No, I don't work. I'm going to school for cosmetology. I'm opening up my own salon when I finish."

"I do hair too. I used to own a salon before I got older and couldn't stand on my feet that long. I specialized in natural hair, cuts, quick weaves, color, and perms."

"That's dope Dro didn't tell me that. You could teach me a few things."

"I sure can. So why don't you work? How do you provide for your daughter?"

"My daughter's father he lives in Ethiopia, and he provides for us."

"Okay, that's nice. I never worked either my husband was a businessman like my son he provided a nice life for me too." Giselle, Kassence and I got to know each other while we ate, it was nice. I didn't get the gold digger vibe from her. She was pushing a nice 2017 Porsche Cayenne. I had to call Dro to make sure he didn't buy that because I wanted one my damn self.

I can't wait until my husband gets out the FEDS he's been gone for twenty years. He'll be home in a few months. Let me call Kaniya it's so not like her not to answer the phone, and she hasn't returned any of my phone calls.

"What ma what you want, why do you keep blowing my phone up? I'm mad at you, can I be mad at you and call you in a few days to bug the shit out of you?"

"Kaniya watch your mouth before I drive over your house and beat your ass and dare your husband to jump in?"

"Dang, why do you want to beat me up all of sudden? I heard you had lunch with your daughter in law?"

"How you know? Stop talking to Dro. I actually like her."

"Whatever Ma. I like her too."

"If you say so, I'm sorry about yesterday I really am. You and Dro both got on my last fucking nerves. I'll be so glad when my husband gets out, so he can take me away."

"I'll be glad too."

"What are you trying to say?"

"You need some dick."

"What makes you think I'm not getting any?"

"Ugh, ma I don't want to know."

"Look heifer don't do me. Just know when my husband comes home I'll be out of the country for a few months and you won't be able to reach me."

"You deserve it. You know that you can't get rid of me and you'll miss me. Just because you got a new daughter in law, don't get shit confused and start acting funny I'm not having that shit."

"Kaniya, I'm your ma always now, I know you're mad at me, but watch your damn mouth. I'm still the adult our relationship will never change no matter what. Let me get up off this phone. Come by the house tomorrow so I can see my babies."

"I will." I love Kaniya she'll always have a special place in my heart. To be honest, I can't wait to get to know Ms. Giselle, a little more too. I haven't seen her and Dro together, but I can tell just by looking at her and picturing him that they'll look good together.

I hope she's the one for him. I want him out of the streets bad, and he knows it. His father will be home by April, and he can't stress enough that when he comes home, he wants his son home too and out of the streets. Dro is just like his father and that shit scares the fuck out of me.

I told his father that Dro would change when he was ready, but he has too want it for himself. If Giselle's the one for him, he'll change a lot of his ways for her. If Dro is serious about Giselle, he needs to let his son's mother know. I've never been fond of Chanelle, but I tolerate her because she's my grandson's mother. She rubbed me the wrong way, and I knew she wanted Dro for only what he could do for her. She hasn't worked a day in her life, went to school for a trade or anything.

I didn't raise a fool he knew better to make her anything more than what she already was, that shit wasn't happening, and she was disrespectful as fuck. I had to smack her a few times because she got out of line.

Just because I'm an older woman don't mean shit. I'll bust your ass like your mother should've.

Giselle

I'm so tired of motherfuckas judging me. I can't win for losing. I swear I feel like smacking a bitch. I was talking to Journee on the phone, and Nikki was yapping in the background talking about hoes don't change. I knew she was throwing shots at me. I kept telling Journee to put Nikki on the phone.

I'm sick of her. I've never done anything to her. She's never liked me. All I ask is for some respect. I've never disrespected her. Kaniya and I were going to lunch at Pappadeaux this afternoon. I told Dro that I would bring him some lunch back. I didn't hear her knock on the window. I unlocked the door and pulled off into traffic. Pappadeaux wasn't too far from here. I was so stuck into my thoughts I didn't even say anything to Kaniya until we were seated at the restaurant.

"Hey to you too. Dang Giselle, what's wrong with you?"

"Everything."

"We can do lunch another time."

"You're fine."

"What's wrong, talk to me?"

"You sure you want to know?"

"I asked, didn't I?" I gave Kaniya the rundown of everything that's happened. She wasn't speechless.

"I thought my life was wild. Fuck her don't kiss anybody's ass, and never let a bitch disrespect you. You're a pretty dope person. I like you for some reason. The only person that should be mad is Alexis. The Nikki girl needs to find her something safe to do if you never fucked her man. Everybody has done some hoe shit. I know I have. I'm not ashamed of nothing I've done."

"Tell me about it. It's a Christmas party Friday. Alonzo and Alexis are throwing it. Dro invited me, do you want to come with me? I wouldn't ask you, but I don't want to be all up in Dro's face if he's with his boys. I definitely don't want to be clinging to Journee if Nikki and Alexis are on some bullshit."

"Alonzo, he's cool I met him before. I don't know Giselle. I don't even like females like that. I'm surprised I like your ass. If a bitch says one thing wrong to me, I'm liable to empty a clip in a bitch's face."

"Kaniya chill out. It'll only be for a few hours. If you ain't feeling it, we'll leave."

"Who said I was going?"

"What do you have planned?"

"Nothing I might go to Miami this weekend to see my mother."

"Come to the party with me, and I'll take you to Miami next weekend on me."

"I'm bringing my guns."

"No guns it's not that type of party."

"Any party I go too. I'm carrying."

"Kaniya leave that shit at home, can you fight?"

"That's an insult. I need to teach you a few things since bitches want to speak recklessly about you and think it's okay to do so. I'll be honest with you Giselle if I go I should bring my gun because if I bring my knife. I'll butcher a bitch, and you'll have nightmares."

"Bitch you're crazy. It's a house party, and it's a few pregnant women that'll be there."

"So, you like crazy bitches. In that case, the pregnant bitches' better keep they mouth shut. I don't mind chin checking a bitch. House party or not I'm carrying something. I don't trust motherfuckas." Oh, my God Kaniya is crazy. I pray Nikki and Alexis don't let anything slick roll out of their mouth, I swear I felt so safe around her.

I wouldn't let her bring a gun to the party if the tension was that bad we'll just leave. I knew Kaniya could hold her own it wouldn't be a Tyra situation and I refused to take any more ass whooping's. Kaniya and I finished eating our food we had two drinks. She was a breath of fresh air. I swear my day went from bad to great in a matter of minutes. A lot of people probably think like, how can you be friends with your man's ex? It's simple because I'm grown ass woman.

I don't have to dislike or be jealous of any female because she dated a guy that I used too. I'm very confident about where I stand in Dro's life, and he's making sure of that. He reassures me every day that I'm the only woman that he wants and needs. I dropped Kaniya off at her suite and pulled up at Dro's. She wanted me to straighten her hair Friday for the party. I needed a hug from my man before I went home.

"You back already baby?"

"Yep."

"Come here."

"I only stopped back by for a little while. I brought you your food. You know I should get going. Kassence needs to be picked up from school. I'll head home to cook, and clean too. I wanted a hug before I left I had a rough day. Are you coming by once you close up shop?"

"Do you want me too?"

"You know I do."

"Meet me at my house, you and Kassence can stay there tonight. Stop by the store and cook whatever you were going to cook at my house."

"Okay, I'll go home and get the stuff. I still have to get her some clothes for school tomorrow." Dro walked up from behind and swooped me into his arms. I swear he's the sweetest, how can you not love a nigga like this? I got him wrapped around my fingers, in an effective way. I love him so much. I swear to God I do.

***

Chapter 11

<u>Giselle</u>

There's some hoes in this house if you see them point them out

There's some hoes in this house if you see them point them out

"Giselle is that you?"

"Yes, Mrs. Simone it's me in the flesh."

"Bitch who is that old lady that's with the shit?"

"Girl that's Juelz momma and God momma Valerie Nikki's mother."

"Oh, the two of them old hoes are with the shit. I noticed before we walked in they were playing Jeezy, and as soon as the two of them saw you, they changed the song up and started laughing and pointing at us."

"Girl don't pay them no mind. They're a hot ass mess. Mrs. Simone beat my ass a few months ago after

Juelz found out that Kassence wasn't his. Let's go stop by and say hey, and mess with them, messy ass."

"Okay, show me Juelz so I can see if I know him."

"I'm not, I don't want them to think I brought you here to bag somebody's nigga."

"Fuck them."

"Be nice, please. I'm not ready to get thrown out just yet and ruin a perfectly good outfit fooling with you and your theatrics."

"You know I'm not nice, but for your sake and the Christmas spirit. I'll try but do know that I'm ready to turn up at any time. Let's take a few shots, so I can be a little tipsy to be around these people that I don't know, and if I have to pop off, I can blame it on the alcohol."

I haven't even been in this party for a good ten minutes, and Simone and God momma Valerie are acting a damn fool. I should've known something was up. Simone is a fucking drunk on the low, and God momma Valerie is a hot damn mess.

I walked up toward the DJ booth, Simone, Valerie, and that other lady Troy that's always with them, where keeping up some damn mess. The only person that was missing was Shanden. Simone was mixing up some of her Moonshine and eggnog, and Valerie called herself being the fucking DJ. I can already tell that tonight is probably going down in the history books fooling with them.

Kaniya and I made our rounds I introduced her to a few people that I knew. Dro and Alonzo flagged us down. Smoke threw his hand up. Skeet and Juelz nodded their head at me. I'm not with the fake shit anyway; they didn't have to speak I'm not pressed at all. The only nigga that I was pressed for in the room was Dro. None of the niggas in here are weighing up to him, and he's all mine. I love when he swoops me up in his arms. He had the softest lips. He couldn't keep his hands off me.

"Ugh get a room."

"Whatever, you good?"

"Yeah I'm good." Kaniya walked off and let me and Dro talk for a few minutes. I had the whole room watching us, ask me, do I give a fuck? Dro doesn't care where we are. We light up the room when we're together.

"I missed you."

"I see, I'm proud of you tonight. You handled those two like a lady should. I saw it on your face that you were ready to say something slick, but you held your composure."

"Thank you; I tried to turn the cheek I didn't want to ruin the party."

"You want me to body a nigga tonight huh? This is a Christmas party; did I tell you that you could wear that shit? You smell good too. I want you, can I have you later tonight?"

"Whatever Dro stop playing. If I get enough of Simone's eggnog mixed with moonshine, I'll fuck around and rape you tonight."

"I'm not playing, you know I'm crazy as fuck about you. I got something for your ass too, coming out the house, without no panties covering my pussy. I can tell when you ain't got no panties on."

"It's easy access, and in case you're ready to come on down tonight."

"Keep playing with me, and I'm going to take everything that you're offering."

"That's what I want you to do. You got me out here feenin for just a little bit."

"You ain't ready Giselle; I promise you're not."

"I am." Dro and I finished talking until Kaniya walked back up. I wanted to chop it up with my man all night, but that's rude because I brought her here. We made our way toward the kitchen where Journee and her crew were kicking it.

I noticed all eyes were on us as soon as we walked up. I hope and pray nobody says nothing out the way because Kaniya is a little firecracker waiting to pop off.

Nikki

Giselle walked into the Christmas party with some bitch. I had to do a double take. I know this hoe didn't bring another hoe with her, so she could steal somebody's man. Giselle was smiling with not a care in the world. I could tell that Dro was really feeling her, and she was happy. I still didn't trust the bitch. I noticed Alonzo gave the girl with Giselle a hug. I nudged Alexis to see if she saw that.

"Bitch I'm watching."

"Oh okay, I'm just making sure."

"Journee, why did you invite your little friend here?"

"Nikki, I didn't. In case you forgot she's dating Dro, so of course he invited her." Giselle and the chick made their way over to where we were sitting. I rolled my eyes I just couldn't stand her. Even though Journee had Juelz, I still didn't want the bitch around. They should've killed that bitch in Africa with everybody else.

"Hey, Journee and Alexis. Hi Nikki." Everybody spoke except me. I don't do fake shit. If I don't fuck with you, there's no point in me faking it. The girl kept looking at me, and I looked at her.

"I thought they said no hoes allowed." Everybody got quiet. I wish a bitch would say something, so I could slap some sense into her. Giselle spoke up.

"Nikki, I don't know what's your problem, but you're using that hoe word too loosely. I've never done anything to you. Last I checked I never fucked your man, so I don't understand why you would have an issue with me."

"Giselle don't come up in here talking shit and get your ass whipped because your side kick is with you, she can get this work too. Just because I'm pregnant ain't shit changed I'll still get ignorant and a fuck hoes like you and her up. In my book, you'll always be a hoe. Journee and Alexis can be cool and cordial with you, but I won't. I see right through you."

"Nikki I'm not taking an ass whooping from you or anybody. You got me fucked up. I'm sick of you. It's ok for you too disrespect me and call me out of my name, but as soon as I say something back, you want to fight."

"Of course, I want to fight because I don't argue with hoes or bitches like you. I lay hands on you."

"Excuse me, but my name is Kaniya last name, Miller. I've done plenty of hoe shit, point your nigga out and ask him, have I ever been a hoe for him? Unlike Giselle, I'm not explaining myself to no bitch, not even you. I don't know how ignorant you think you are, but if your pregnant ass wants to throw some hands let's go because I'll beat your child clean the fuck up out of you."

"Bitch you don't want none of me."

"Nikki, chill out you're pregnant for God sake."

"No Alexis, if she has an issue pregnant or not I'll solve it."

"No bitch, you don't want none of me. If you want to fight, we can do that. Let me take my shoes, coat, and jewelry off. I'm not with disrespect. I can show you better than I can tell you. You don't even have a real reason to not like this girl. She ain't never did shit to you. Why do you want to fight her because she stood up for herself? Fight me. You're a fucking bully."

"How you know?"

"Because she fucking told me. The only person that has a right to not fuck with her is Alexis. She hasn't fucked your man."

"She'll fuck yours."

"Any bitch that has ever fucked some dick that I have papers on, she isn't living to tell about it."

"What's that supposed to mean?"

"Just like it fucking sounds. Figure it out." I don't know who this chick is that Giselle brought with her, but I like this bitch she doesn't give a fuck. She took her shoes and coat off she was ready to fight.

"Come on Kaniya let's go, too much drama and bullshit."

"I'm ready it's sad, that this woman doesn't even have a real reason not to like you, she wants to show her ass, and her home girls won't even correct her when she's wrong."

<u>Valerie</u>

Alexis and Alonzo invited me to their Christmas party. I wasn't going to go, but Simone insisted that I come because she was coming. I like Simone, but when she gets drunk, she does a bit too much. I came through anyway though. Alexis wanted me to be the DJ, and Alonzo wanted Simone to be the bartender.

Some shit will never change. I'll be so glad when Nikki's miserable ass have those babies. She's getting on my last fucking nerves. I can't take it. Skeet ain't making shit no better he lets her do whatever the fuck she wants. I've never met a pregnant woman who I literally wanted to smack a few times.

Simone and I watched Nikki, and ole girl go at it. It's funny how history repeats itself. Kaisha and I go way back. I met her the same way Nikki met her daughter. I took one look at her when she walked in the door, and I knew that she was her mother's child.

Oh, my God, it doesn't make sense how much she looks like her mother. Killian didn't do any work at all. You couldn't get Kaisha up off that dick. Let me go stop these too crazy girls. Kaisha was a firecracker. Say one thing that she didn't like, and she was popping off.

"Y'all two are doing too fucking much. This is a Christmas Party."

"No, you and the old lady started playing that song when we walked in the door and started pointing at us."

"Don't disrespect my mother."

"I'm not; my mother raised me better than that."

"Speaking of your mother, I know her."

"Oh, you do?"

"Umm huh very well, I took one look at you. If you ain't Kaisha in the flesh; I don't know who is, watch this." I pulled out my cell phone and hit the Facetime button to call Kaisha we go way back her, Julissa and me.

"What's up Valerie what you want? You and KD already set my ass up with Khadijah."

"Damn shut up; you talk too much. Look who I got with me." I put Kaniya on Facetime.

"Kaniya what the fuck are you doing with Valerie? Don't believe the shit she tells you about me unless you heard it from me."

"Ma I'm at Christmas Party with Giselle."

"Be good Kaniya don't let Valerie get you drunk. Valerie look after my damn child, make sure she gets home safe and don't tell none of my fucking business."

"Bye Kaisha, your business is public record."

"I told you I knew her. Nikki and Journee, Kaniya's mother, used to hang tuff with Julissa and me back in the day. Kaisha was from the Eastside, she ran Eastlake, Edgewood, and Kirkwood, and we had the West on lock Bowen Homes and Bankhead Courts. I met your mother the same way you and Nikki just met. Are you the twin that's married to Lucky or Yung?"

"Lucky."

"That's my daughter's first cousin. Her father and Cynthia are brothers and sisters"

"Ugh, I can't stand that bitch."

"Watch your mouth; I can't stand that bitch either. I beat her ass a few times. Ask your momma, so yes, we're family by marriage. Journee's sister and brother's father Big KD and your father are cousins."

"Oh, God. I know Big KD."

"Yeah, you and Nikki need to squash whatever feud y'all had. Hug it out that's what your momma and I used to do. We used to stay at it. Y'all family blame Killian for y'all not knowing each other." It was good seeing Kaniya; she reminded me of her mother. Kaisha would show her ass anywhere. Kaniya and Nikki are one in the same, that's one fight I wouldn't want to see. If Kaniya is anything like Kaisha with the K, I know she's packing something. It's in her DNA.

Chapter 12

<u>Giselle</u>

The Christmas Party was a hot mess. Kaniya and I were a little tipsy, but I could drive us both home. Dro said he would meet me at my house in an hour. Of course, I couldn't wait to see my man and lay up.

"Thank you for coming out with me tonight. I really appreciate you for having my back."

"Girl, it wasn't a problem. Nikki got you fucked up. I have so much shit going on, I was ready to fight to relieve some of the stress that I have."

"I see, has your husband came back yet?"

"No, he hasn't, but I'm okay. I actually had fun despite the little drama."

"Do you miss him?"

"Of course, I do, but I'm okay with being by myself. We've been together for eight years, and the last two have been hell. Normally if I was going through this and I wasn't married, and children were involved. Bitch I would've bagged me a nigga the next day just because, I know I've grown up because that hasn't crossed my mind at all. The only thing I want to do is love on my three. Jamel, Jamia and Jeremiah are everything to me."

"I guess we do have that in common. My last two niggas weren't shit. More the reason why I was skeptical to fuck with Dro. I want another baby so bad, I don't think I can have anymore."

"You'll have another one, keeping busting it open and watch what happens. Dro is a real nigga I can vouch for him. He's in love with you. If you would've seen Dro about eight months ago, He's a totally different nigga. I'm so happy that he found someone that can calm the savage and beast that lies inside of him."

"How do you know?"

"He told me."

"I'm in love with him too. I swear to God I am. The way I feel about him. I've never felt this way about any man before. When we first me, I was a little skeptical because of everything that happened to me. It's like God kept telling me he was the one. I felt it."

"I'm so happy for you. You deserve it. I can't wait to feel like you feel again. I'm going to pray that baby fever rains down on you."

"You will." Kaniya and I chopped it up until I made it to her house, she didn't live far from me. I watched her get inside of her house. She called and let me know that she was good. I pulled off and made it home in no time.

***

Dro was waiting for me in the driveway. I don't know why. He had a key. I pulled into my garage and cut my truck off. He walked up behind me and bit the nape of my neck and grabbed a handful of my ass. I turned around and looked at him. He pinned me up against my truck. I could tell that he was drunk I smelled the liquor on his breath. He lifted my skirt up.

"How did you get all of my ass in this skirt?"

"The guy at the mall helped me get in it."

"You're going to stop playing with me. You won't be satisfied until I kill a nigga." He carried me into the house and up to my room. Dro and I were making out and tonguing the fuck out of each other. I wanted him so bad. I hate when he gets me all hot and bothered.

I just want him to put the tip. The freak in me will bounce on that dick so hard. He wouldn't have a choice but to fuck me properly.

He tossed me on the bed, and I bounced a few times. He snatched my skirt off me and ripped my blouse off and just looked at me.

"I want it; I promise I'll be a good girl." I tooted my ass up and looked at Dro and bit my bottom lip. He smacked my ass so hard. I know I have a hand print on it.

"I want you to be a really bad nasty girl when I give it to you." Dro had no clue what I had in store for him when we took it there. His dick was hard it was saluting me. He's going to regret holding out on me. Y'all think I'm hoe watch me be a hoe in the sheets for my nigga.

"Go home Dro so I can put in some work with this rubber dick."

"No rubber dick tonight. I'm drunk as fuck. I'll fuck around and get pulled. You know you want me to lay here with you."

"I do, but I'm hot and bothered, and the only thing that I want lying beside me and between my legs is you. If we ain't fucking, take your ass down stairs. I'll make good on my promise tonight and rape you."

"My baby can take it, can she?" Dro pulled my body toward the edge of the bed. He unfastened my bra and tore my panties off with his teeth. His tongue trailed the insides of my legs. He started sucking on my pussy. I started squirming I didn't know what he planned on doing to me.

"Don't move you hot and bothered right? Get up here and ride my face so I can put that flame out. You better not fall either."

"Whatever."

Dro didn't have to tell me twice. I stood up in front of him and threw my legs over his shoulders. He went in for the kill. I could barely keep my composure. My legs were weak. He kept smacking me on my ass. I promise you I would've raped his ass tonight if he would've laid next to me, and I didn't get any sexual attention. I don't want to be a virgin again. I wanted my man to beat this pussy out the frame. I'm tired of these little mind games that he's playing.

My body shook I had multiple orgasms back to back. Dro knew what the fuck he was doing the whole time he was eating my pussy I was moaning, and he was laughing at me because I was sexually frustrated. I wanted to smack him in the back of his head; his tongue felt so good and the way he lapped up all my juices.

I couldn't right now, but in the morning. Who told him to try some new shit with me, we've been dating for a few months now. It's time to explore each other sexually.

Dro

Giselle and I have been going real strong for about four months now. I'm ready to make her my wife. I introduced her to my two sons about a month ago, she was good with them, they liked her, and she loved them as if they were her own. I should've introduced Chanelle and Giselle to each other before I let Giselle meet them. So, before I make it official with Giselle. I'll introduce her to the mother of my children Chanelle.

I rather break the news to Chanelle myself before she hears it from anybody else. She keeps her ears to the streets when it's pertaining me. Chanelle and I never had a relationship. We used to fuck from time to time. When I didn't want to fuck different broads, I would fuck on Chanelle somehow in the process I slipped up, and she got pregnant. She has two things that matter the most to me Roderick and Rodarius.

I haven't fucked Chanelle in a minute, it's been about eight months. I had to stop fucking her because she kept pressuring me to be with her. I didn't want my sons to see me running in and out of their mother's house, and we weren't in a committed relationship.

I had love for Chanelle, but we couldn't be together. My best friend Yadi he got killed about five years ago, in a home invasion. He used to fuck with Chanelle, but they weren't together when he died. It was me, consoling her when he died, she ended up coming on too me, and we fucked. She always had a thing for me and on one of my many drunken nights. I took her down through there.

Lord knows I felt bad about doing that shit, but it happened. Chanelle had a daughter by Yadi, and she had my two sons. A lot of our niggas didn't agree with it, but it is what it is. Yadi's mother thought I had him killed because of me and Chanelle fucking around. Yadi and Chanelle wern't together when he died. He was with Olivia.

"Dro I'm ready." Giselle walked up behind me and wrapped her arms around my stomach.

"I'm ready to baby."

"What if she doesn't like me?"

"I'm not worried about if she doesn't like you. Nobody is going to stop me from being with you."

"Okay." Giselle's worried about the wrong shit. Who cares if Chanelle doesn't like her?

We're still going to be together no matter what. Chanelle knew that I was coming to pick up my sons for the weekend. I didn't tell her that I was bringing Giselle. I didn't need too because I pay the mortgage on her house and the note on her car.

I called Chanelle to let her know that I was on my way. Giselle hopped in, and I closed the door for her. We pulled off in traffic. Giselle grabbed my hand she had a habit of doing that when she felt like I was stressed.

"I love you, Giselle."

"I love you so much more Dro." Giselle was the sweetest female I've ever known. Free and Juelz were dumb if you asked me. I don't know how they ended up letting her slip through the cracks; I'm glad she let a boss ass nigga step up and show her what a man is supposed to do.

***

We made it Chanelle's house forty-five minutes later traffic was hectic. Lil Dro called my phone at least five times to see when I was coming. I told him that I was on my way. I put my truck in park and opened the door for Giselle. We walked hand in hand up to Chanelle's door. I rang the doorbell. Chanelle opened the door she had her robe on leaving little imagination. Giselle squeezed the shit out of my hand.

"Dro who, the fuck is this and why are you bringing a bitch to my house?"

"First, watch your fucking mouth, her name is Giselle not bitch, she's my fiancé. Go put some fucking clothes on. Don't walk around showing half your ass when my sons are here. Last I checked I paid the mortgage on your house."

I could already tell that Chanelle was on some good bullshit. I hope she didn't think that I was coming over to fuck. I could tell that Giselle was mad. I would have to explain some shit later to her. She snatched her hand from my hand so quick. She was in her feelings and now wasn't the time for it. I grabbed her hand and forced her to hold mine. She was rolling her eyes and sucking her teeth. I could tell that she was mad.

Giselle hasn't seen the rough and aggressive side of me. Chanelle finally came stomping down the steps. I don't know what her problem. For her sake and not mine, she better not be on no bullshit because, I would handle her ass;

she knew it was. I hate to say but it was just a fuck thing, but I got my sons in the process.

"What's up Roderick? I guess you're not Dro today."

"Look Chanelle. I didn't come here for no bullshit or no extra shit. I wanted you to meet Giselle's because she's permanent in my life and our children will be around her."

"Dro, what made you think that it was okay for you to bring Giselle to my house? Ask me first, don't just do it. My sons are too small to be meeting any females that are not related to them. Just because you brought her over here to meet me, doesn't mean that I'm comfortable with her around my two."

"Chanelle cut the bullshit. I've fucked with a lot of women. Count on your fingers how many you've met because I wanted them to be around my sons."

"It doesn't matter Dro I'm not comfortable with it."

"Normally I wouldn't get involved with baby momma drama, but I'm not going anywhere Chanelle. I was once a bitter chick like you too. It's not about you being comfortable. It's about me being with Dro. Real niggas do real things, he didn't have to introduce us, but he had enough respect for you to do so. I have a child of my own, and I would never do anything to your two children. Since I walked through the door, I showed you nothing but respect and trust me I wanted to act real ignorant the way you came to the door, showing your ass."

"Daddy and Ms. Giselle, we're ready to go."

"Dro, how do they know her already? Lil Dro and Rodarius go back upstairs to your room. Y'all aren't going anywhere." I see now that Chanelle is trying to make it real hard for a nigga because it ain't no us. I'm glad I cut the dick off months ago,

"Giselle go out to the car. I'll be out in a few."

"No, I'm staying right here Dro, whatever you need to say to her I want to hear it."

"Giselle, go the car please, some shit you don't need to hear."

"Why?"

"I'll explain it to you later."

"You heard what the fuck he said. I'm tired of looking at your big pie face ass anyway."

"Chanelle shut the fuck up." Giselle did what I told her finally. She was in her feelings; she slammed the door hard as fuck. I'll have to some ass kissing to get in her good graces.

"I see you still like bitches that you can run."

"Chanelle watch your fucking mouth. It ain't never been you, and it'll never be you. You were just a fuck and convenient pussy. You knew what it was. When you see, Giselle watch your fucking mouth. Don't ever call her a bitch, because you'll regret it and I'll start treating you like a bitch. Make yourself comfortable with seeing her. My sons like her and soon enough they'll love her the same way I do. Go get my son's it's the weekend and their rolling with their daddy."

"Dro you got me fucked up. How dare you bring a bitch to my house and flaunt her in my face like I'll accept it because I don't. I was good enough for you to fuck and suck when you wanted me too, but you couldn't at least give me a shot.

I asked you time after time was there anybody else and you said no. I had to hear it from the streets that you were fucking off with somebody. You're passing out titles like I'm supposed to agree with it.

We messed around for five years, and I gave you two sons, and this is how you shit on me?"

"Chanelle we can never be, you fucked with my nigga Yadi strong. I stopped fucking you because you kept asking me to be with you. I didn't want to keep getting the pussy and for you to have hope that it could be something. You have his daughter and let's be honest bitch you trapped me. I took you to the clinic to get an abortion and what you do?

Bitch you lied like you handled it. I don't regret my sons, nor do I regret you having them. I regret that I was so fucked up and raw dogged you. I regret that I paid you money to kill my seeds. I regret that. I've never misled you that we can be anything more than what we are.

I always told you when I meet the right bitch you'll meet her and be prepared. You laughed that shit off. Since you want to be in your feelings, get you a job and pay your mortgage and your car note, because I don't have to do it. The only thing I have to do is take care of my two."

"I'm sorry Dro. It's just hard seeing you with somebody that ain't me. Why wasn't I good enough? Why couldn't we be together for the sake of our two kids?"

"Chanelle, sometimes shit ain't meant. Maybe it was meant for you just to have my sons, and that's it. Do you know how many bitches I fucked, and they never got knocked up by me? Don't worry about the why's worry about you.

It's somebody for everybody, and I wasn't that nigga for you. Go get my son's so I can roll." I had to check Chanelle because it needed to be done. Chanelle is my son's mother but Giselle is about to be my wife, and I don't ever want Chanelle to think it's okay to disrespect her because it's not.

Lil Dro and Rodarius came down stairs with their bags. They kissed their mother goodbye. I walked to the truck and I noticed Giselle was gone and my shit was just running. I fastened them in their car seats. I called her phone at least ten times, and she didn't answer. I knew she was mad, but she didn't have to leave.

We were supposed to be staying the night at my house.

I love Giselle, and I let her get away with a lot of shit, but this little stunt she pulled I got something for her ass. I couldn't even drive how I wanted too because my sons were in the car.

Why would she do that? That's so disrespectful you didn't even tell me that you were leaving, and now you're not answering your phone. I get that you're trying to make a point. I swear she wants to see a side of me that she doesn't need too.

Chapter 13

<u>Giselle</u>

Dro and Chanelle got me all the way fucked up. I had to leave he was in her house entirely too fucking long. I don't like how he dismissed me. I didn't even bother to fight with him. I just left, to make matters worse, this bitch was so disrespectful.

I wanted to ask Dro when, was the last time he fucked her because he ain't fucking me. I'm sexually frustrated. The moment I walked in the door the tension was real for what though. I can't stress it enough I'm so tired of bitches disrespecting me.

Is it a sign on my face saying fuck with Giselle because she ain't gone do or say shit? I can't catch a break for shit. I called me an Uber. Towne Center Mall wasn't too far from here. Shopping was therapeutic for me. Kassence could always use some new stuff.

Before I called me an Uber, I called Journee, and I could hear Nikki and Alexis in the background. I told her that I would call her back. I called Kaniya to see where she was; she said that she was in the area and she would scoop me.

She was right on time. Kaniya picked me up in front of True Religion. It felt pretty good for it to be the first day of winter. It was 70 degrees.

"Thank you for picking me up. Where are the babies?"

"Girl, my father has them. he has them so spoiled. I go to his house just because, he'll baby sit. Where too?"

"Your house, I'm not ready to go home yet."

"Are you hungry?"

"Duh."

"Let's eat, what you want?"

"It doesn't matter."

Okay cool. I'll cook something because I need to wrap some gifts." Kaniya was really a nice person once you got to know her. We rode in silence. I cut my phone off because I didn't want to be bothered. I knew Dro would be calling me.

My mother had Kassence. I called to check on her while I was shopping. I could tell that Kaniya was going through something. She was singing her heart out, and tears escaped her eyes out, and she didn't bother to wipe them.

Since I met her if I called her, she would answer, and she's been there for me if I needed her.

***

We finally made it to Kaniya's house. I could tell that her house was nice, just by looking at the outside of it. When I stepped inside, I was blown away. Her home was nice as fuck. It was beautiful.

"Your home is really beautiful."

"Thank you." I looked around. She had a beautiful family. She and her husband looked good together. Kaniya called me to the kitchen. She poured me a glass of wine. She started preparing our food which consisted of pepper steak and rice.

"What's wrong Giselle?" I gave Kaniya the rundown of everything that happened.

"Giselle, let me keep it real with you. God puts people in your life for a reason and a season. You and I cross paths for a reason. I don't know why, but we did and had nothing to do with Dro. I know exactly how you feel.

I never got the chance to apologize to you for how I acted when I first met you. I'm sorry I should've never pulled out a gun on you. It's a reflex that I need to work on. I never believe in making the same mistakes twice, but somehow, I always end up doing so.

Trust me I'm learning from my mistakes. I just met you, and so far, you're an amazing person. You're a heart is made of gold, and a lot of people may not see that, but that's okay everybody might not get you, but for some reason I get you.

Never let anyone disrespect you. I don't give a fuck who it is. Respect is everything, and I'm willing to die for mine. It's hard for me to turn the cheek and ignore some shit, and that's bad, but I'm working on me. I love to fight I'm a fighter, but it's not about winning or losing it's about standing up for yourself and not going out.

Correct me if I'm wrong. I don't think you should've left. I know you were upset and in your feelings, but you should've waited it out. It maybe some stuff that you didn't need to hear. Just ride for your man. Just trust him."

"My trust is so fucked up. It's so hard."

"Mine is too. Everybody isn't out to hurt you. You admitted that being with him feels different. I don't think God would bring you this far to let you down again. Don't ruin your chance of happiness by being focused on the wrong shit. It's not healthy."

"I'll try."

"Do it, hurry up and eat your food. So, I can take you home."

"Why are you trying to get rid of me?"

"I'm not, but you have a man to go home too. Instead of running from
your problems. The two of you need to talk it out."

"So, what about you, what are you going to do about your husband? You
have a beautiful family. Don't throw that away."

"You're on the outside looking in. I can't talk about this shit right now. Whatever happens, happens and I'm okay with that. I'm far from perfect by a long shot, and I don't want to be. I'm telling you all of this because I don't want you to make the same mistakes that I did.

I ran away from everything, and I refused to talk about issues that I had. I'm in this situation because of some shit I did." Kaniya and I finished eating, and she took me home. It was good to talk to someone that has an open mind and not judge you.

***

Kaniya lived about twenty-five minutes from me. We made promises to see each other soon. I really hoped her, and her husband works it out. When she talks about him, her face lights up. I had to use my door key because I didn't drive. I walked in my house. I cut the living room lights on, and Dro was sitting on the sofa waiting for me. My heart dropped. We locked eyes with each other. I could tell that he was mad as fuck with me.

We needed to talk I didn't expect him to be here waiting for me. I'm a little tipsy from the wine. I needed a hot shower, and to forget about what happened earlier. I didn't even acknowledge him that's something that I never do. I'm just in my feelings; he should understand where I'm coming from. She was totally disrespectful, yes, he checked her a couple of times but so what.

Dro and I have never had an argument since we've been dating. I don't know how this little incident would play out. I shouldn't let it get to me, but I was pissed. I wanted him to sweat and feel the absence of me not being present. I could've behaved differently, but she's a grown ass woman she knew better.

He was hot on my heels dying to grab me. I put a little pep in my step. I wanted to get to my room and close my door before he could stop me.

Chapter 14

<u>Dro</u>

Giselle had me hot as fuck. Literally, I'm pissed. I asked her to do one thing, and that was to wait in the car, but that was too much for her. She wanted to be nosey, and she didn't need to be. I called her phone over ten times. I know she cut it off.

I called Kassence to see if she had heard from her, and she said that she had. Kassence was spending the night with Giselle's mother. We were supposed to stay the night at my
house, but Giselle had other plans. I picked up Kassence up from Giselle's mother house brought her home with us. I fixed the kids something to eat and put them to bed.

Giselle walked in; it was a little after 10:00 pm. We locked eyes with each other. Giselle didn't say anything to me. She walked straight upstairs to her room, and I was right on her heels. As soon as she entered her room, I tapped her on the shoulder. She turned around and looked at me.

"What's up with you? Is this how you're doing shit now?"

"What did I do wrong Dro? I waited on you for a long time, and I couldn't come back in because I wasn't wanted there. So, I caught me an Uber to the mall to clear my mind, and a friend picked me up, and we had dinner and drinks." She turned around and walked away. I grabbed her waist to stop her, and I pulled her close to me. I had to smell her to make sure she didn't have any cologne on her. So far so good.

"Friend and drinks?"

"Yes, a friend."

"You better stop fucking playing with me. What you did was wrong, and you and I aren't rocking like that at all. Do you trust me, Giselle?"

"It wasn't a guy. I'm not on any hoe shit. It was Kaniya, yes I trust you to a certain extent."

"Giselle, did I accuse you of being a hoe? I don't give a fuck what you did before me. The only thing I care about is what you do while you're with me. If I had a feeling that you were a hoe, baby I would've never pursued you. I would've beat that pussy up between your legs months ago.

Trust me, when I say that I would never shit on you. Have faith in me. I know you've been through a lot. I can promise you that everything you've been through its stops with me. I don't want to do, what the last nigga did to you. I'll walk away first. Know your position in my life. Have confidence in where you and I stand. I haven't fucked Chanelle in months. I don't want her at all. I had to break that shit down to her plain and simple, and I didn't want you too hear me talk to her like that."

"How many months?"

"Over eight months. I'm not fucking nobody Giselle."

"I had to ask because you're not fucking me. I'm a woman, and I have needs. Of course, I'm feeling some type of way because she came to the door with her ass out and no panties on ready to bless you with some pussy. I haven't even had the chance to do it."

"I understand where you're coming from, but I corrected her immediately. I never lead her on to think that maybe she had a chance with me. I wanted her to know that it's Giselle and Roderick. She has to respect that because you're not going anywhere."

"Okay, I'm sorry Dro for running off."

"You want me to hurt you, don't you?"

"Why would I want you to hurt me, Dro?"

"You're playing with me. You know I'm crazy about you. I care about you. I promise, you captured a boss's heart these past few months. Don't ever cut your phone." I grabbed Giselle's hands and put it to my heart, so she can see how it beats when were together.

Giselle was sexually frustrated that's why she was acting out. I got something for her. I know she has needs, shit I have them too. I'll handle her needs tonight. Since she keeps putting it out there. I'll handle that ache between her legs. I followed her to the bathroom; she undressed right in front of me.

She knew what she was doing I sat on the toilet seat. I placed my face in my hands battling with myself. I swear she's making me go against everything I said I wasn't going to do. I'm already gone off her without the pussy. I know when I get it I'll be a certified fool. Our relationship wasn't based on the sex, that'll be a bonus too. She has needs, and I damn sure want to be the only nigga fulfilling them. I don't ever want it to be a thought in her mind that I'm fucking somebody else that'll never be the case.

The shower was running for a good five minutes. I'm sure the water is perfect. I started undressing myself prepared to get in with her. I snatched the curtain back and stepped in. She looked at me, and I looked at her. I grabbed the soap out of her hands and took control of washing her body from head to hoe. I was using this shit as an advantage; she said she had needs let me do my job and fulfill them. I washed every hole of her body and to make sure that it was clean to my liking. I had to taste it. My tongue is dangerous each time I tasted a hole on her body, her body shook.

"Baby can you stop please." She moaned.

"You have needs let me fulfill them." I cut the shower off. Giselle tried to run out of the shower first. I stopped her before her she could get another foot out. I grabbed the towel and dried me and her both off. I carried her to the bed and placed her in the middle. I locked the door; I didn't need the kids busting in. I never had plans to fuck Giselle. I wanted to make love to her. I've fucked a lot of women, but it's not one bitch out here that could say that I've made love to them. I grabbed the Shea butter off Giselle's dresser. I made sure her whole body was moisturized.

"Dro."

"After tonight call me Roderick." I started at the bottom, and I planned on working my way to the top. I sucked every one of Giselle's toes. She had the prettiest feet they were well taken care of. I ran my tongue up both of her calves. My hands and lips enjoyed caressing and kissing her thighs. I sunk my teeth in both of her butt cheeks. My face finally made eye contact with her pussy, something that would forever be mine.

I threw her thick chocolate thighs over my shoulder, smacked her on the ass twice. I dug one finger inside of her she was tight as fuck. Virgin tight I'm going for the kill always. My mouth was dangerous I tried to tell her that. One slurp and she started squirming.

She started touching my head. I know she was enjoying it. That was just the warm up. I started sucking her pussy real foolish. I wanted her to feel my tongue all of it. My face and tongue were buried so deep, I bit her folds and shook my head like a dog.

My tongue was still assaulting her pussy. Her juices were fucking up these sheets. She's a soaker. I knew I had her she started backing up and running. I placed my hands on her legs to stop her.

"Stop please, I can't take it," she moaned.

"You have needs remember? You're a grown ass woman take what I'm giving you." I eased up on the head. I had to make room for the dick. I let my tongue play a little game with her stomach. I had her body covered in chills. Her titties were sitting up, nipples extra hard waiting for me to suck them big chocolate motherfuckas. I knew Giselle was nervous, her body tensed up.

My dick was already brick hard. I slid the tip in and a soft moan escaped her lips. I took my time with Giselle she wanted it so bad. I had to give her inch by inch. She started backing up as I started filling her up with this dick. Now isn't the time to be running when you're constantly throwing it up in my face about you have needs.

"Giselle be still, I promise I'm going to be gentle with you." I continued doing what I was doing. She placed her hands on my chest. She was looking at me with her big eyes begging me to slow down and stop. She knows I'm a sucker when she pouts her lips. We started kissing so she could stop worrying so much. The kissing was intense.

"Dro do we need a condom?"

"For what, you ain't about to be fucking nobody, but me. Stop talking to me and let my do my thing. Be careful what you ask for now you're getting scared." Giselle thought she was slick she started laughing. She feels so good I had to put my mind on something else because this pussy was extra warm, and too fucking wet. It felt too good, and I'll bust quick.

"I'm not."

I put that pound game on Giselle. I was stroking my pussy long and hard she had tears in her eyes. I had to place a pillow behind the headboard, so the kids couldn't hear us. With each stroke she started backing up, and her titties kept bouncing and hitting me in my face. I placed my hands on her hips. Sweat was dripping off my forehead.

"Let me ride you."

"Do your thang." Giselle got up there I sat with my back up against the headboard and my hands behind my head. She started playing with my dick. Her head was face down between my legs, and her ass was tooted it up, she went crazy sucking the tip of my dick. Next thing I know I felt my dick at the back of her throat, she gagged a little bit, but it was sexy.

She started humming on it like a bird. I knew I was about to cum if she kept on. I hope she wasn't watching my feet. My toes were curled, and I couldn't be still. I wanted to moan, but I refused too. I bit the inside of my jaw instead. I started smacking her on her ass, so she could stop. I wasn't ready to bust yet not in her mouth but in her pussy.

"Get your ass up here and ride this dick like you asked to do." Giselle was sneaky motherfucka she thought that shit was funny. She turned around and jumped on my dick and started riding it. I smacked her on the ass and grabbed both of her titties and matched her rhythm.

She thought this shit was a game. I'm a savage in the sheets. I flipped her ass on her backside and dug deep off into her walls; she was hollering. She better quit playing with a nigga like me. Her juices were running down the crack of her ass. She had my dick covered. I placed my hand over mouth. I whispered in her ear.

"Take it."

"I am."

"I want you, face down ass up." She did as she was told. I grabbed her hair and pulled her body close to mine. She was throwing it back on a nigga; she had me going insane just watching her from the back. She did this little thing with her ass cheeks that drove me insane. We both had something to prove. I'm the plumber and I slang nothing but straight pipe.

"I'm about to come," she moaned.

"Let that shit go; I'm coming right behind you."

I kept going for the kill until she said that she was about to come. We came together. I know we just went half on a baby.

I went into the bathroom to get soap, and a towel to clean myself and her up. By the time I made it back to the bed, she was knocked the fuck out. I started cleaning her up anyway. I wanted her to change the sheets they were soaked we couldn't sleep on these.

"Giselle, baby, wake up, so we can change the sheets."

"I'm tired."

"I know it won't take long." She got up and sat in her recliner and laid down. I changed the sheets out myself. I placed her back on the bed and tucked her under the sheets. I was tired too. She scooted her ass up on me.

"Let me know if you want me to wear you out again." She backed up quick. I laughed and wrapped my arms around her waist and pushed up right on her.

"I love you, Roderick."

"I love you too Giselle."

"You better." It was after 12:00 am. Sleep took over Giselle instantly. I was right behind her no blue balls tonight.

***

Chapter 15

<u>Giselle</u>

What a night. I'm on cloud nine, and I don't ever want to come off. I'm very satisfied Dro took care of me, and I'm good I should've acted out sooner. He busted all up in me. I'm in love with him. I can't help it. I started crying because when Juelz and I were together he wouldn't even let me touch him, while we were having sex.

Dro was a different nigga; he was a real nigga. He was gentle and passionate with me it was crazy. This man-made love to me. I'm experiencing things that I never had. He took my body to new heights. I can tell that he really cares about me.

I can't believe he went to pick up Kassence too. I didn't even know the kids were here until they knocked on the door this morning because they were hungry. I got up and fixed everybody some breakfast. I guess Dro got her straight, because she was very sincere about her boys not being around me.

I'm not going anywhere at all. I see why she's crazy behind that dick. If he fucked her, how he just fucked me, I'll be doing the same shit, not.

Dro and I needed that conversation, because clearly, that bitch wanted to fuck my man. I know I use to be a fool back in the day over a nigga or two, but damn Chanelle cut the cake she wanted to get fucked literally. I wanted to hear what was said. I love Dro's sons like they're my own.

Enough about this bitch let me fix my kids and king some breakfast, so can create some more memories. It's the weekend, and I don't want to do anything but lay up with my little family or whatever. Bacon scrambled eggs with cheese oatmeal, biscuits. Dro was still asleep. I know I turned his ass out last night. He couldn't take the head that I was giving him. I didn't want to tease him last night, but today it's a different story.

I let Kassence scramble the eggs. Lil Dro placed the bacon strips on the skillet. Rodarius placed the biscuits in the pan. I had the water boiling for the oatmeal. It wouldn't take long for the food to get ready. I had Kassence take the boys upstairs to wash their faces. She considered them as her little brothers.

I went ahead and started setting the table. The bacon aroma started to smell throughout the kitchen. I felt a pair of strong arms wrap around my waist. I looked up, and it was Dro.

"What you are doing up so early?"

"I was looking for you. I wanted you to handle this morning wood, but you ran off on me. I knew you were all talk."

"Whatever my babies were hungry, so I had to fix them and my king some breakfast."

"Oh, I'm your King now?"

"Umm huh." Dro started sucking on my neck and whispering in my ear what he wanted to do to me. I almost collapsed in his arms. I was so turned on.

"Don't fall I got you."

"Move you play too much." He started laughing. The kids came running back down stairs.

"Daddy Ms. Giselle let us help cook."

"Did she?"

"Yes, I'm hungry." Dro tried to finish helping me cook. I made him stop I got this. The food was practically done. We had a few more minutes on the biscuits. I started preparing the plates, so the kids could start nibbling away. I cut up some fresh fruit, the oatmeal needed to cool off.

Breakfast was finally ready, and everything was at a decent temperature for the kids to eat. I could see myself getting used to this. Having a blended family isn't bad. I got baby fever I want another baby bad too another girl. Dro is the perfect father.

***

<u>Giselle</u>

Dro and Alonzo went out of town to handle some business for the weekend. I had a few things to do. Kassence was invited to a sleepover. One of her friends from school was throwing it. I might stay the night with them. I was missing Dro something serious; he's only been gone since Thursday. I'm so used to him holding me even if it's only for a little while. I'm craving his touch.

Dro and I went over Alonzo's and Alexis's house. Alexis was there she just threw her hand up, and I was okay with that. I understood it, but I didn't respect it. Dro asked me what was going on and I told him nothing. If she didn't want a relationship; I was okay with that, just because I was at her house. I didn't have to smile in her face.

I let Dro and Alonzo do what they needed to do. She wasn't a saint she admitted to cheating on Free throughout the relationship. Kaniya's going to the mall with me later. We've become really close these past few months.

I had to finish getting dressed, and we could be out.

We decided to go to Lenox and Phipps that was perfectly fine with me because that wasn't too far from our homes. We can eat at the Cheesecake Factory when we're finished. Kassence didn't need anything I didn't either. I needed to get my iPhone fixed and a new Apple Watch. I dropped my phone and copped me a new Apple Watch.

Kaniya wanted to go in Bloomingdales. I love Bloomingdales I'm an addict in that store. I came across a few things that I could use. Kaniya was getting some lingerie and perfume and a new bag. I noticed the change in her. She was on her phone the whole ride here, and she had a glow to her. I wanted to ask her about it.

"Damn you're looking quite happy. Your husband came back?"

"No, he's still gone. He doesn't have anything to do with my happiness."

"Okay did you meet someone?"

"No, I'm doing a few things that I'm really excited about. Even though Work Now Atlanta is practically new.

I'm getting it gutted out. I'm redoing the whole office space. Which means that everything that my EX had access too. He no longer has that. All of the cameras that shit has to go."

"I'm happy for you. You needed new lingerie to celebrate?"

"Thanks. Mind your business Giselle, yes, I needed new lingerie. I'm doing a photo shoot really soon." Kaniya and I finished talking. I grabbed me some new lingerie also. I decided to get Dro a few things. I heard a familiar voice, I didn't pay it no mind until the voice got closer.

"I heard she was a hoe too. I don't know what he wants with her. I can't stand the pie face bitch." Kaniya looked at me, and I looked her. I sure she caught the aggravation on my face.

"Do you know these hoes?"

"Yes, one of them is Dro's baby mammy."

"Which one?" I pointed her out, and Kaniya rolled her eyes.

"Never let a bitch disrespect you behind your nigga. Check that hoe once, so you won't have to check her again."

"Okay." I understood what Kaniya was saying. We paid for our stuff and left Bloomingdales. My phone should be ready by now. As soon as we hit the exit, Chanelle and four other girls were waiting on us.

"If that bitch on some slick shit. I don't give a fuck where we're at, handle it. Don't worry about how many trust me I got the other three."

"What are you saying?"

"They're on some bull shit. Just watch." We finally approached the exit and they were still there. Chanelle stood at the exit trying to block me from exiting. I pushed that bitch out of my way with so much force, she almost fell. I'm tired of bitches trying me and calling me a hoe.

"Watch it." I didn't pay that hoe no mind I kept walking.

"That's my bitch, right there. I wish a bitch would." Kaniya was with the shit. I hope Chanelle ain't on no bullshit, because I swear I would give it to her the worse way. Dro would be mad at me.

We headed to the Apple Store. I got my phone, and we were good to go. Chanelle was standing right outside by the Apple Store. Kaniya gave me that look, she always gives. It was six of them now.

"If those bitches follow you to your truck. I'm catching a body."

"Are you carrying?"

"What do you think? I hope you are too, because I'm tired of telling you."

"I'm carrying."

"Good because you may have to make an example out of a bitch," I swear Kaniya is crazy; she lives to shoot a bitch. I thought she was all talk. Chanelle continued to follow us, talking shit. We laughed all the way to the car. I finally made it to the garage. I threw my bags in the trunk. Kaniya stood right beside me, grilling these hoes.

"Do we have a motherfucking problem? I'm trying to figure out why you're following me?"

"Problem, bitch you're the fucking problem. I do what the fuck I want to do because I can. I don't know if

Dro ever told you, but he can't control me. I do what I want, and I don't care about him giving you any title. I'll fuck and suck that nigga when I want too. It's not that easy for him to cut me off. He's going to continue to pay my bills and by me whatever the fuck I want. We're sharing that nigga; you need to fall in line hoe."

"Chanelle you're silly as fuck. I swear I used to be just like you. I grew up though. The difference between you and me are. If I had to check any female about my nigga, it's because she was out of line, and didn't know her place. I never came at you sideways. Since you met me it's been a problem. Get out of your feelings it's somebody for everybody, but Dro is for me.

Dro is a good nigga, BUT he's my nigga. I'm not sharing shit, that dick belongs to me. His heart belongs to me. I'm the only bitch, that's going to be fucking and sucking on my nigga.

As far as him paying your bills and taking care of you. I'm putting a stop to that because you're getting shit confused. He provides for you because you have his two sons nothing more nothing less."

"You got the game wrong. You're not about to stop Dro from doing nothing that he's been doing for me."

"Watch me."

"Giselle, come on I'm hungry this bitch ain't talking about shit. Don't argue with this bitch about your man, and he's never been that to her. She's a bitter baby mother, nothing more nothing less." I slammed my trunk closed and attempted to walk to my truck, as soon as I was about to open the driver's door.

I felt my hair being yanked, and a pound to my head. I turned around, and it was Chanelle and one of her friends. Kaniya jumped out of the truck, and it was show time. The other girl that was on me, Kaniya got her off and slammed her face into the pole.

"If y'all bitches want to fight her, it's going to be fair. If anybody jumps in, I'm shooting a bitch dead in their fucking head. Fuck with her if y'all want too." Kaniya wasn't playing with these hoes today. She had two guns cocked ready to air this bitch out. Chanelle could fight, I'll give her that, but I was hanging with this bitch.

She wanted to fight me behind my nigga, more of the reason for me to beat her ass behind my nigga. I refused to take another ass whooping. She kept hitting me in my beautiful face, and it kept pissing me off. I punched her in the stomach twice and knocked the wind out of that bitch. I picked her old trifling ass up.

Momma Edith taught me how to kill a bitch with two fingers. I grabbed her by the windpipe and squeezed it. She started choking. I applied more pressure to her wind pipe, her eyes started to turn blue. I released her, and she fell to the floor. I kicked her in her head and stomped her fucking teeth out.

"Get this bitch from behind my car, before I crush her fucking legs."

"I'm so proud of you. I thought you were about to kill that bitch I was ready to layout the other four."

"Thanks, I know I'm hip, no face no case."

"Good you are learning something. What are you going to tell Dro when he hears about this shit?"

"The truth."

"Okay. Don't say that I was with you because I'm known to be a trouble maker to some people."

"If it wasn't for you, all five those bitches wouldn't have jumped, and it's no telling how this whole incident would've played out."

"True, you know as long as I'm with you. I'll never let a bitch try you. Never question that." Kaniya and I went to eat at the Cheesecake factory. As soon as we sat down, and our food came. Dro was on my line, asking me what happened. I explained myself, he said he was on his way back, and I better be at his house by the time he makes it home. He had to get his boys. I could tell that he was a little mad, but she started fucking with me. I just finished it.

"I'm sorry Kaniya. Dro was going in, what's wrong?" She gave me her phone to look at it. I just shook my head I couldn't believe it."

"You wanted to leave me. I'm totally fine with that. I've accepted it. If you wanted to fuck off with this bitch, cool I'm okay with that too. The moment that a bitch and your momma get besides themselves to inform me of what's going on all bets are off. Take me to my house now."

"Kaniya calm down. Fuck that shit."

"It sounds good Giselle. I wish I could say fuck it. I'm a changed a bitch, but I haven't changed that much. A bitch gone feel me today. I'm going home to change clothes, and I'm pulling up at Lucky's momma's house.

I guarantee you this nigga is going to regret the day he even looked at me. I don't care about what you are doing. If a motherfucka go out the way to let me see it. They're going to regret it."

"Please don't go to that lady's house. I can't let you do that. Never go to somebody's house."

"I'm not the one to brag, but trust me, when I do pull up at Lucky's momma's house the coroner is coming they're carrying out two motherfuckas. Yirah and Cynthia, me and Lucky will be the last one standing, and if he wants to shoot it out, then we can do that. Don't play with me that's all I ask. Play with your kids."

"I thought you wanted to change and you were tired of doing that behind him? Let that shit go Kaniya, please. You have three beautiful children who need you. I know you're pissed off but guess what that nigga knows you. His momma and that bitch know you too. They're expecting you to pull up and show your ass.

Don't give them the benefit of the doubt. I said months ago that I'd never go to a bitch's house. I'll make an exception for you because since I met you, you've been down from the start and I've never had to question whether or not you'll ride for me."

"You're right, but I don't want you to go against what you said because of me. I would never hurt him intentionally. This is one of the main reasons why I'm glad that he's gone. He'll try to hurt me just because, Giselle I'm a crazy bitch, and I can admit that. I will kill his momma. Out of all the females that Lucky has fucked with.

I bodied every bitch. I left Yirah alive for a reason. I knew she couldn't stay away from him, and I knew he couldn't stay away from her. I put this on my momma. I'll chill for today, and I'm going to change my number. If this shit ever comes to my phone again. I'm killing him and her. I'm not afraid to be a single mother."

"What am I going to do with your crazy ass? I'm going to pray for you and Lucky for the sake of y'all kids. I'm a single mother, and I have only one. Lord knows Free done a lot if shit to me, and he deserves everything that came with it." We finished chopping it. I dropped Kaniya off at home. Dro has called me five times already asking where I was.

Chapter 16

<u>Dro</u>

Chanelle and Giselle are running me crazy. I had a business meeting with my connect in New Orleans. Alonzo and I left Thursday. I wasn't supposed to come back until Sunday. This final business meeting was to solidify me leaving the game, that's why I had to make the trip and turn everything over.

Alonzo was my right hand, and everything was in his hands. If he needed me, I would lend a hand. I'm done with the game and I'm going to clean a lot of this money I've been saving over the years. I couldn't even enjoy my last night here. I was ready to get back home anyway I was missing Giselle's ass like crazy.

Alonzo wanted to go to the strip club. I haven't stepped foot in a club in a minute. Giselle was everything that I needed in a woman. The women were beautiful they didn't do shit for me because I knew what I had at home. My lusting days were over. My phone rang my mother called me and told me that I needed to come home quick. She had my two sons because Chanelle and Giselle had a fight. Chanelle was in the hospital.

She was my child's mother true enough, but I was more concerned why Giselle hadn't called me and said shit.

I told Alonzo I was taking an early flight some shit popped off back home. He was cool with it, and we left. New Orleans to Atlanta was a six-hour drive. I was making it in three. I was mad at Giselle she knew better. She better be at my house by the time I make it. I'm an hour away.

***

I finally made it home. Alonzo dropped me off we slapped hands with each other. Giselle's truck was parked in the garage. I unlocked the door, she wasn't downstairs in the living room. I walked upstairs to my room; she was in my bed looking at the TV.

"Hey, baby."

"Hey, are you okay?"

"I'm fine." I started undressing and climbed into bed right beside Giselle.

"You naked."

"Yep." Giselle knew what she was doing. I picked her up and laid her on top of me.

She started playing with my dick, getting my shit hard, instantly she put my dick inside of her.

"Tell me what happened," Giselle explained everything that I happened. I'm not surprised at all. Chanelle needs to let it go. It ain't her it'll never be, and she knows that too.

"Are you mad at me?"

"No, but I don't want the two of y'all fighting. She started it with you. I always want you to defend yourself no matter the situation. Go ahead and finish what you started. We have to go get the boys from my mother's."

"Okay."

"Keep on you're going to end up pregnant."

"I can't have no more."

"Are you fixed?"

"No."

"You haven't been fucked properly by the right nigga, you know I'm the plumber I'll dig deep off up in your shit and bury my seeds there."

Giselle can't stay off this dick she'll fuck around and be pregnant soon. I warned her already. It ain't no pulling out. I swear she rides my dick the best. I'm tired too I couldn't wait to get back home to this.

Chanelle's mother called my phone. I don't know what for, she never cared for me. My mother had my kids. I wasn't going to the hospital to see Chanelle the same bitches that boosted her ego, to fuck with Giselle better be there to have her back.

I let Giselle answer it, and she hung up. I wasn't about to fuck my nut off for nobody. She needs to tell her daughter to get out of her fucking feelings and move on. Giselle cut my phone off and we got back to us.

***

Chapter 17

<u>Giselle</u>

Life has a funny way of showing you things. I swear these past few months I've been so happy, It's the happiest I've been in a very long time.

I felt relaxed and stress free. My hair was growing. My melanin was popping. I've gained a few pounds in all the right places.

I was doing great in school. My cosmetology instructor wanted me to be the head stylist in class. My daughter was happy. Dro was amazing, and I love the way that he cares for my daughter as if she was his own.

He wants to adopt her and give her his last name. I'm open to it. I've came a long way since last summer. It's crazy how your past will come back to haunt you. I'm not a saint, and I'm not ashamed of anything that I've done. Sometimes in life, you'll go through certain things to get to where you're going.

Ugh, my EX. I can't even say that he was my first love. Snake is being released from prison. I met Snake when I was fifteen years old. I would never forget this, long as I live. I met him at Greenbriar mall. I used to see him around the way. He would always look at me, and I would look at him, but we never said anything to each other.

He finally approached me one day at the corner store, we exchanged numbers, and it was on from there. When we first got together, he stole my heart instantly. This man brought me everything.

He picked me up and took me to school every morning. He let me drive all his cars.

When your young dating an older guy with money, that was the life, so I thought. I've always been attracted to older guys. On the outside looking in he had it all. Money, cars, clothes and too many fucking hoes.

I was young and dumb when I was fucking with him. Snake was so fine, every bitch wanted him, and they could have him too because he didn't care that I was his girlfriend. If a bitch wanted to fuck him, he'd be glad to give them the dick, and he'll take the pussy and tell me about it later.

He burned me one time. He was my first, and I wasn't having sex with anybody but him. I told him about it. He beat the shit out of me because I confronted him about it. I lied to my mother and grandmother that a few females jumped me.

I knew then that I didn't want to be with him. It took my body a week to heal. He came by the house to check on me, acting like he really cared. My grandmother and mother loved him. I despised him he couldn't have a better name besides Snake.

As soon as they would let him in my room, he would beat me, if I didn't let him fuck. He would stuff his fists in mouth.

I hated him. The best thing that happened to me is when he got cased up on a home invasion. Nobody knew, but I flattened his tires when him Ry and Caman went in that house. Ry and Caman rode together, but they left before him.

Snake was greedy he didn't want to ride with his boys because he had other plans. He went in and out of the house at least four times. I'm glad he was solo because I didn't want his boys to get locked up with him. I flattened his tires and called the police. I watched them lock his snake ass up. I laughed so hard when I walked back home. I just knew that things were finally about to look up for me.

I made it back home. I took a hot shower I was waiting on Snake to call me. Two hours later no call, but I received a knock at my door. My mother opened and said that some girl was at the door for me. I opened the door it was Sade this mixed chick that everybody was telling me that Snake was fucking with.

I'm grilling this bitch, and she's grilling me. I was only seventeen at the time. This nigga was foul for real, do y'all know this bitch had the nerve to ask me for 14,000 that my man left here. I looked at this hoe and laughed. I slammed the door in her face, did she know, or did he think that I was that dumb?

Snake was pissed because I didn't turn over his money and weed to her. I changed my number. I was through with him. On the outside looking in Snake was the perfect nigga. He looked good, smelled good. The sex was good too. I was so glad when he got locked up. He had a hand problem. He would lay hands on me if I looked the wrong way. If he caught another man looking at me, he would swear I was fucking them because he was fucking off.

I don't know how he got my number, but he called me the other day and told me that he needed his money, or it was going to be some problems. He was getting out. I have 14,000 that's change to me, but was I going to give it to him. Hell, no I'm not the same sixteen-year-old that he used to beat senseless. I would kill ass if he tried that shit with me.

Dro and I are honest with each other. I never mentioned Snake to him because he didn't matter but sense he's making threats.

I'll have to tell him what's going on, so he won't to be in the blind about anything that's going on. I hate to wake Dro up when he's sleep, but it's important.

"Baby wake up for a minute." I placed soft kisses on his lips.

"I'm tired, Giselle."

"It's important normally I wouldn't wake you." Dro got up from the bed to wash his face and brush his teeth.

"What's up baby, tell me what's so important?" He walked up behind me and wrapped his arms around my waist. I gave Dro the rundown of Snake and me he tensed up a little bit. I grabbed his hands.

"Why am I just now hearing about this?"

"We dated when I was younger, and I didn't think it would matter."

"It definitely matters if he's making threats to you. Fourteen thousand dollars ain't shit, and you don't have to pay him, he needs to charge it to the game. I'm going to buy you a new phone. Give everybody your new number. I'm waiting on his pussy ass too call back."

"Promise me you want to do anything crazy?"

"I can't do that Giselle because I take threats to heart. I will kill a nigga for threatening my family. I need you to know how much you and Kassence mean to me." He grabbed my face so that I could look at him. Out of all the niggas that I've been with I never have to question Dro. I know where we stand. I can conquer the world with him.

<u>Dro</u>

Giselle has been really stressed out these past few weeks, with school and this Snake nigga. I told her that I had her and to trust me. Of course, I asked around about this lame ass nigga; he wasn't about shit. It was pissing me off that he was threatening her. She feared him because he used to beat on her. I really wanted to kill his ass just off the strength that he did that. We had money I could pay him, but she's not paying any fucking body.

I had her phone, and he kept calling, as soon as I would answer he would hang up. I knew it was his pussy ass. Alonzo told me if I was looking for him. I could catch him off Cleveland Ave. posted up, and his momma stayed in Jonesboro.

I'm sure we'll run into each other soon. It ain't no limit what I'll do for Giselle. My mother had the kids so of course, I wanted to do something nice for her. We had reservations at The Main Event, she didn't want to go she claims that she was tired, she just wanted to lay on me.

We needed to get out of the house even if it was just for a little while. It was cold as fuck outside too. I picked her up and placed her in the tub. I ran her a nice hot bath.

Giselle would give me any excuse, not to go anywhere. So, to avoid her saying that. I took matters into my own hands and got her everything that she would need to go out with me tonight. I had her clothes out for her already. Kassence helped me out.

"Baby this is nice, you didn't have too. We could've stayed in the house. I don't care about all of the extra stuff as long as I'm with you I'm good."

"I know Giselle, but I wanted to take you out and do something since we're kid free. I want to show you off. Let me spoil you."

"You spoil me enough Dro. It's cold outside, and I'm allergic to the cold. I want your body heat to keep warm. I just want to lay up under you with no distractions."

"You're going to fuck around and get pregnant laying up under me."

"What you don't want me to have your baby?"

"Don't put words in my mouth, that's not what I'm saying. Of course, I want you to give me another child, but I have some other plans first, and you keep making a nigga detour and change what I have plans I have in motion because you have needs. Whatever Giselle finish washing up because we have dinner reservations at 9:00 pm."

"It ain't my fault; I don't see you complaining when you're getting head for breakfast every morning."

"I'm not complaining. I love it when you're face down ass up. I love watching you from the back when you're taking this dick that I'm giving you."

"Act like it." Giselle and I finished talking; she continued to wash up. I started getting dressed putting my clothes and shoes on, so we could leave. 9:00 pm would be approaching soon. I don't want to be late; I'm hungry as shit.

Chapter 17

<u>Snake</u>

Time ain't on a bitch side when my fucking money is involved. I've been gone for eight years. Giselle had my money and weed. My niggas thought I should charge it to the game, but I wasn't. The day Clayton County hauled a nigga off and threw me in the back seat and cuffed me. I did the crime, so I was prepared to do time. I wanted my shit. I knew I was going to be gone for a while and I was okay with that, but I wasn't okay with her having my shit.

I sent Sade to her house to get everything. Giselle didn't know that I was fucking with Sade. She heard, but she wasn't for sure. I had thirty thousand at Sade's a little of that went toward my attorney's fees, and to take care of my kids that I would be leaving behind. I needed that money so Sade could pay my connect, and she could re-up for me, and make my money while I was in jail.

Giselle was dumb, so I knew that she wouldn't have a problem with turning over my shit. She fooled a nigga she didn't give Sade shit, and she changed her number on a nigga a few times. I was salty, but I wanted my money. I kept tabs on her from behind bars. I was her first everything. I heard she fucked with niggas that had money and she was well off. All that shit was cool, but the bitch needed to pay me. I'm putting interest on my shit since she's wealthy.

I'm tired of waiting I need my money to make some shit happen. I've counted this money already. It ain't no way around it. It wasn't a gift you were holding my shit for re-up purposes. I've been watching her for a few weeks, but she didn't know it. I knew where she laid her head at I even knew what type of cars she drove.

Every time I would call her phone that nigga would answer. I didn't say shit because my issue wasn't with him, he didn't owe me she did. If he wanted to save the hoe okay, but run me my bread, tonight, was the night that she was going to feel me.

I had my nigga Ace put a tracker on that phone it was pinging at The Main Event and guess who's pulling up? Me I want my shit nothing more nothing less. I'm about thirty minutes way hopefully this shit goes smoothly because a nigga is still on parole and I'm not trying to get sent back.

Giselle

We made it to The Main Event. I've never been here before. I have so many first with Dro it's amazing, he introduces me to so much. I love it our relationship is so exciting and refreshing. Dro ordered us some food and a few drinks of course.

I'm not really a drinker I only drink with him. Dro and I were sitting at our table holding hands and talking. We looked up because we notice that we had company. It was Snake before I could even address him, he let some slick shit roll off his tongue.

"What's up bitch? I need my money."

"Excuse me."

"I got it from here Giselle, aye partner you need to watch your fucking mouth when you're speaking to her. She's not paying you shit pussy. You can move around."

"It ain't that easy my nigga, I want my fucking money, and I'm not leaving without it."

"Snake you can leave because I'm not paying you shit." He smacked me, and my lip busted. Blood started seeping out the corners of my mouth.

"You done fucked up now nigga," before I could even get up to clean my mouth. Dro got up out of his seat, and rushed Snake. They started fighting I didn't want this to happen at all. Oh, my God, Dro was killing him with his bare hands. I wasn't going to stand there and not help my man because he was protecting me at all cost. I got up to help Dro.

"I got it, Giselle, take this gun and put in your purse." Dro continued to beat Snake's ass a couple of niggas tried to jump my man. I picked up a chair and smashed one in the head. It's not going down like this at all. Fuck Snake he deserved that ass whooping. Tables were thrown, chairs were scattered everywhere. The other people in the restaurant were screaming, the police were called. They took Dro and slapped some hand cuffs on him.

"Excuse me, officer; he didn't do anything. We were having dinner, and the guy over there smacked me."

"I understand Ms. I'm taking Mr. Shannon to jail because he's a convicted felon and he's in possession of a fire arm."

"It's my gun it fell out of my purse and he picked up and gave it to me."

"Mr. Logan stated that Mr. Shannon pulled a gun out on him and he's willing to testify in court after he receives medical treatment at the hospital."

"You can check the camera's that never happened. Mr. Logan assaulted me; we have reservations here. He walked up to our table and started this altercation."

"I understand. I'm doing my job, and that's taking Mr. Shannon away. If everything checks out properly than he'll be released soon, but as of right now he's under arrest because management requested it, and he assaulted Mr. Logan."

"What about him, is he going to jail also? He assaulted me look at my lip and face?"

"Mr. Logan is injured he has to go to the hospital to get medical attention, I can't discuss what will happen to him right now," I swear to God this night went from good too bad in a matter of minutes.

Dro shouldn't be going to jail, and he didn't start it. How dare Snake play the victim when he started all this shit. He lied on Dro; he didn't pull a gun out on him. Since Dro and I have been together, all his guns were in my name. I didn't want him to catch a gun charge being a felon. I walked up to Dro while the officer had him in hand cuffs and kissed him. I wrapped my arms around him. They had him caged up like he was an animal and he wasn't.

"I'm sorry Dro."

"Don't be you didn't do anything wrong. I love you no matter the outcome. I'll do that shit again." I started crying the police pulled me off, Dro. I couldn't take it. He didn't deserve this shit. It's all my fault. I knew the type of nigga Snake was if I paid him, he would've wanted more money. I called Kaniya I needed her.

"Kaniya, I need you now they took him." I cried.

"Calm down Giselle, who took him?"

"The police, we were out eating, and Snake pulled up acting crazy. He smacked me, and Dro lost it."

"Where are you I'm on my way?"

"The Main Event."

"Giselle, calm down, please. Call my mother and wait for my call. I love you, stop crying. I'll see you soon." Those are the last words that Dro said to me as he was thrown into the backseat of the police car. I had to get myself together. I just couldn't believe this shit happened like this. I love Dro with everything in me. I know he wanted me to be strong, but I would rather trade places with him because it's my mess that has landed him in jail.

I couldn't stop crying. Tears clouded my face; my shirt was soak and wet. I knew for a fact I had some lines on my face because my make-up was freshly done, my heart hurts so bad. How am I supposed to explain this shit to his mother and two sons let alone Kassence? I could barely talk. I knew Snake wasn't shit, but this the lowest that he could possibly go.

I grabbed my phone out of my clutch to call Mrs. Rodica my hand was shaking. I hate I have to even make this call. I had Dro's phone and wallet and his keys. She answered on the first ring I could hear my babies in the background.

"Hello."

"Mrs. Rodica I'm so sorry." I cried.

"Giselle, stop crying. Call me Momma let that Mrs. Rodica shit go. Dro already called me. We're family, and I'll never judge you. I got your back no matter what you're not alone out here. Ride with my son the same way he'll ride for you. Stand ten toes down with him. No relationship is perfect. Of course, I don't want my son in jail, but it is what is."

"What am I going to tell his son's and Kassence?"

"The truth."

"This is all my fault."

"Giselle, don't beat yourself up about it. You'll worry yourself sick, and Dro wouldn't want that. We have more issues at hand. The best revenge is to get your man out of jail and show Snake that you're not the one to fuck with."

"Momma why won't he just leave me alone? I told you how he used to beat me senseless. Is it a crime for me to be happy and in love with Dro?

I never gloat or do anything, but damn I deserve Dro. I've got it wrong for so long, and now that I finally feel like that I've got it right, and somebody wants to take that from me." I cried.

"Please calm down Giselle. I understand where you're coming from. Trust me I do. You and Dro deserve each other. People will be jealous and envy of you just because, if you're happy let the fucking world know. You must be doing something right if they're talking.

I want you to get some rest. Tomorrow we can go see Dro to see what they're charging him with and what steps we need to take to get him from behind bars."

"Okay, momma. I'll see you tomorrow. Kiss my babies for me." I felt a little bit better after talking to Rodica. I love the relationship that we have. It's not forced everything felt so natural with her, I know she got my back.

Dro

Snake thought he could smack my bitch, bust her lip and live to tell about it. That nigga couldn't have known about me. He's doing all of this over 14,000 I piss 14,000 When he approached the table, I told that nigga to back the fuck up and move on. He was on my time, and I don't tolerate disrespect at all. I guess he assumed my words didn't mean shit.

I had a feeling that we would run into his ass tonight. He was so disrespectful I would never let anybody disrespect Giselle. I lost it, she was my future wife and soon she would be the mother of one of my unborn. I know I'm a convicted felon I didn't use the gun, but I had that Glock on me. I gave Giselle the gun, and that pussy ass nigga told the cops, what I did, and he was pressing charges against me.

I swear to God a nigga was trying to change and I'm man enough to admit that Giselle is one of the best things that has ever happened to me. She brought out the best in a nigga. I wouldn't change shit that I did. I swear I would lay my life on the line again for her if need be.

The only thing that I do regret is I couldn't wipe her tears when they hauled me off. I just wanted to hold her one last time. I should've listened when she said that she didn't want to go anywhere. It was bound to happen soon or later.

I haven't shed tears in a long time. I shed a few because three strikes and you're out, and I know shit ain't gone look good for a nigga like me despite the circumstances. I never wanted Giselle to cry because of some shit I did. In due time. I finally made to Rice St. Fulton County Jail. I had two calls to make. One to Alonzo and one to Kaniya. The officer shoved me out of the car and walked me inside of the jail to get booked. The orange jumpsuit was placed in my hands.

"Shannon, you back? You got two phone calls make that shit quick." Man, I can't stand that CO. I grabbed the phone I had to plug Alonzo in, so he could know what moves to makes in my absence.

"God damn Dro mane, how you get jammed up, what I need to do?"

"Snake."

"Word."

"Everything is everything, go holla at my OG for me and look after my kids."

"Anything else."

"I'll holla at you in a few days. Put some bread on my books a nigga going to be here for a while." Let me call Kaniya I need her to look after Giselle while I'm gone and make sure she's straight.

"Really Dro."

"Look Lil Buddy don't lecture me, now ain't the time. I need you to do a few things for me while I'm gone."

"What's up?"

"Look after Giselle while I'm gone, she was going through it, when they hauled me off. Show her the ropes with my store so she can run it. Bread her to be a boss, train her, show her what you know, because that nigga ain't gone ease up. I need muscle and make sure it ain't no trace."

"That's it."

"I want her to do everything not you, show her what to do, she listens to you for some reason."

"I hear you. I got you keep your head up. Put her name on visitation, and I'll see you soon." I'll call Giselle once I get booked and processed in. I know Kaniya and Alonzo could hold shit down.

I couldn't let Alonzo get his hands dirty because he's the plug, he has too flood the streets. Kaniya was down, but it wasn't her job to do.

I know she could mold Giselle into being the rider that I need. Snake is coming for Giselle because I'm behind these bars. I need my bitch to protect herself and kill his ass in the process. It ain't no other way I'm not staying behind bars because of this pussy ass nigga. He'll make a move, but when. It's just a waiting game now.

Chapter 18

<u>Snake</u>

If Giselle thought this shit was a game, she's sadly mistaken. I'm a ruthless ass nigga I'm heartless, her fucking tears and the blood that ran don't her face didn't move me. I will kill her momma and grandmother since she wants to play. I want my fucking money, and I'm taxing. I need my shit. I got shit to do and mouths to feed.

It's on and popping now with Dro out of the way. I got some niggas inside Fulton County that'll handle him. After I get finished with her, she's going to wish she paid me years ago. Lord have mercy on her soul, I hope the bitch didn't forget how I used to beat her ass back in the day. I'm the same nigga but older.

She needs to watch, her fucking mouth, and how she talks to me. I'll take her and that nigga for everything that they have. It's hunting season, and she's my fucking prey. I'll sample the pussy to and let that nigga watch.

The police swarmed that motherfucka quick, Sade was waiting around the corner. I got Dro cased up. I saw he had a gun; he was a felon just like me. Yes, he had some nice hands, but I wasn't about to let him have one up on me because his bitch had my money and refused to cough it up.

I won't have any issues getting at her. I haven't put my hand on a female in a long time, but she asked for that shit. It was our business and not his. I asked around about Dro. I knew he was the plug and he had it. If you got it, what's the point of not paying me?

Y'all can call it what y'all want I'm testifying against that nigga. He'll never get out fucking with me. I had to play the victim to avoid going to jail. I'm on parole, and I'm not going back because a bitch doesn't want to pay me my fucking money. I wasn't expecting him to pop off as he did, but it is what it is.

"What now Snake?"

"What you mean Sade, we watch the bitch and catch her slipping and take everything she has. She can do it voluntarily or involuntarily. It's her choice."

"Snake why don't you just leave it alone. We can get up some money another way. I don't see this shit going well. We have four kids to look after and Dro is heavy in the streets, don't you think he'll have somebody looking after her. If he's locked up."

"Sade do you think I'm scared of that nigga? He bleeds just like me; he's not the only nigga walking around here with money and fucking power. Anybody can get touched. Correction bitch I have one fucking child. Your other three kids ain't mine. You made those kids while I was in prison.

I wouldn't even be in the situation if it wasn't for you. I left you 30,000, and you didn't do shit with the money but fuck it off. I'm in debt because of you. You didn't pay the connect or take care of my seeds you tricked off with a nigga."

"I had to pay my bills Snake."

"And if you would've listened to what the fuck I said, you would've been able to do that, but no you wanted to listen to your dumb ass friends and party and bull shit."

Chapter 19

<u>Kaniya</u>

If it ain't one thing, it's something else. My heart broke hearing Giselle cry because they hauled Dro away. I was in traffic on my way to pick her up. Dro was a good nigga. Giselle is like a sister to me; everybody is so quick to judge her not knowing what she has been through. She's a good girl that has been dealt a bad hand, but she's making a way out of no way.

I can't believe Snake pulled that shit. I told Giselle a few weeks ago to slump that nigga because he was threatening her. She thought I was bullshitting. It's all good though because he'll show his face soon thinking he has one up on her. If I'm training her, she's going to rock that nigga to sleep, clean up her mess, and wait on her nigga to come home. So, they could live happily ever after, without a bitch ass nigga in the background.

The Main Event wasn't too far from my house. Thank God Kaisha was in town for the weekend. I had a babysitter on deck. The police had this place swarmed. I valet parked my truck. I jumped out and ran toward Giselle, the police had her in cuffs.

"Excuse me, officer, I got her." Damn, she's breaking my heart looking like this. I grabbed some tissue out of my clutch to wipe her eyes. She broke down into my arms. I just held her in place. If she needed my shoulder to cry on I'm here; I'm not going anywhere. I wouldn't wish this feeling on my worst enemy. I swear I wouldn't.

"Why me Kaniya?"

"Stop crying Giselle, he's coming home, he may be gone for a little while, but he'll be back soon. Dro so gone off you, girl that nigga working as we speak to make his way back home to you."

"How you know?"

"Do you love him? If so, do what you need to do, and make sure that he comes back home to you. I told you weeks ago to kill that pussy ass nigga. You didn't listen, don't let nobody take your happiness."

"You ain't killed Yirah yet, why is she still breathing?"

"Look Giselle, I love you like my sister, but please don't bait a bitch like me. My favorite game is body for body. I got a trigger finger, and I love my sanity right now, this shit ain't about me it's about you and Dro. Don't miss

Dro if you don't have too. I don't miss Lucky I'm glad he's gone. Look at this fresh beat on my face. Check my DM's. I'm good."

"Bitch you just want to be hot in the ass, where are you coming from all dolled up?"

"Yep, there's that smile I love Dimples. I met someone."

"You're playing a dangerous game. Where did you meet somebody at?"

"Who me? I haven't even started yet. I'll show you how real this shit gets one day. If a bitch reaching, I'll snatch hoe soul. It's time to teach Dimples to snatch a nigga soul." I'm glad that Giselle is feeling a little better. It probably won't hit her until she's alone to think about what the fuck happened.

"You're going home, or do you want to stay at my house tonight?"

"Bitch you're a little nice today. You got some dick?"

"Not yet, don't do me, take your ass home in that big ass house."

"I'm just playing I'm coming to your house. I can't lay in my bed and smell Dro, and he's not there I'll die." I don't have time for Giselle and her theatrics we have work to do and bringing her man home is a job within itself.

***

I pulled up to my home. Giselle was asleep on the passenger side. Poor Dimples, she's tired. I woke her up, so she could be prepared to get out. Lucky was parked in the driveway. He couldn't come in. I had the locks changed and the garage code. I don't care if our kids where in the house or not. He wasn't coming in the day he walked out on me and mine it was a wrap. He walked up in the driveway.

"Where the fuck you been and why can't I get in my house?"

"Lucky, you left your house. It's after hours anyway. Comeback tomorrow when it's daylight."

"You got me fucked up; I paid for this shit. I'll see my kids when I'm good and god damn ready; it doesn't matter the fucking time."

"Whatever Lucky I'm not even about to argue with you." I walked off from him. I'm sick of him. I haven't seen him in months, but he wanted to show up today out of all days. I felt him yank my hair. I kept walking. He threw me up against the wall in the garage. He took my phone and keys and emptied everything out of my purse.

"Strip butt naked right here. You want me to beat your ass Kaniya you got me fucked up. I saw you and that nigga. You can't play me. I will fucking kill you. I said I needed fucking space it ain't no moving on."

"Are you finished?"

"Are you fucking listening?"

"You left Lucky, did you actually think that I was about to be sitting around waiting for you to come back. It's cool for you to lay over your momma house and fuck Yirah. Have I come at you sideways about that shit? I'm not tripping you know why because you can keep that bitch.

If a bitch can get anything that I had, I don't want it. If a nigga is comfortable enough to leave his wife and kids and lay up with bitch who I despised I don't want him. Take your ass on I'm good me, and my kids don't need shit from you.

I'm not for the games at all. Tell your bitch and your momma to keep fucking with me, and I'll snatch both of those hoes soul, and your son's soul too. Yeah, I had Jamal tested he yours bitch you covered that shit up good, but you left some shit unturned.

As far as you, paying for this house. I brought you out, your name ain't on the deed to this. I wanted this house; I put the offer on it. You couldn't stand to see me doing something on my own without you. Check your account your money is there, and while you're at it sign those fucking divorce papers."

"You are snooping huh. Yes, he's mine I fucked up Kaniya I did. I should've been honest with you from the jump, but you fucked up too. I'll take care of all my kids. It ain't no breaking up. Do you see how you flipped this shit on me?

I didn't leave you to be with her and my son. I left you because you hard headed as fuck and you want to have these side relationships with these niggas who don't mean you any good. You don't give a fuck about me and my feelings. If it ain't your way, it ain't no way. You'll hurt me anyway you can. You actually thought I wanted to leave you?"

"Lucky none of this shit matters to me right now. I'm tired and despite how you may feel I care about your feelings. All this shit you caused own up to it. Lay in the bed you made. Maybe it's not meant for us.

Jamal being your son changes the game. He is the same age as Jamel and Jamia, you cheated on me in the beginning, and you have a baby to show for it. Every time we have and issue or disagreement you revert to your old ways. I can't stop you from cheating. I'm not enough for you. Push me into the arms of the right nigga because I'm sick of you."

"You don't know when to shut the fuck up."

"I need to shut up now because I exposed you."

He started choking me because he couldn't handle the truth. Niggas can dish it, but they can't take it. He didn't deny fucking her. If I learned anything from being with Lucky, be two steps ahead of him. He shot me when Jamia wasn't his. It hurts that Jamal is his, but why do all of that to cover it. I knew it was a reason his mother would act funny toward my kids. It's all good though.

Chapter 20

<u>Giselle</u>

I didn't sleep too well last night. I was missing Dro like crazy and I had to make sure my girl was good. Her husband is crazy as fuck. I met her mother last night; she was a breath of fresh of air. I was waiting by the door last night to make sure he didn't hurt her. He came out of nowhere going crazy.

It hurt my heart to listen at the two of them go back and forth. Her mom tapped me on the shoulder and said they're going through somethings and she'll be just fine. After that, I went to bed for that reason only. I guess he didn't leave because I heard them arguing and the babies were crying.

Real bitches do real things. I swear to God whenever I call Kaniya she comes hands down; she'll drop what she's doing to make sure I'm straight. In the mist of her going through all of this, she made sure I was good. She has the heart of a lion. I wish I had half of her strength. I felt like the weight of the world was on my shoulders. I miss my nigga like crazy. I heard a knock at my door.

"Wake up sleepy head, are you hungry?" Kaniya walked in with her babies' right behind her. It's crazy her kids are a mixture of her and their father.

"Yes, you know I am. Are you okay?"

"I'm okay how do I look? Jamia and Jamel say Hi to Ms. Giselle."

"Hi." The two of them are so precious, her family is so beautiful. I swear I wouldn't throw this shit away. If it can be saved, I'll try and talk some sense into her.

"That doesn't mean anything, how are you?"

"I'm okay Giselle, come on and let's eat." I followed Kaniya to the kitchen. It smelled good; she had breakfast laid out nice. Her mother was sitting at the counter pouring coffee.

"Good Morning Ms. Kaisha."

"Call me Kaisha."

"Okay." I grabbed me a plate and started to fix my food this shit smelled to good. Kaniya placed the twins in their high chair and started feeding them. Her mother held Jeremiah and started feeding him.

"So, Giselle what's the move, or you are moving in on Snake's pussy ass or what?"

"Excuse me?"

"Girl my mother knows everything."

"I'm saying you need to level the fuck up and make sure it ain't no case against him. Handle it."

"Okay."

"It ain't no okay. Y'all young girls are to chill and relaxed about shit. Snake wouldn't even make it to see the sun rise if he was fucking with a bitch like me. As soon as that nigga hit the corner, it would've been lights out for his ass. He's sending niggas to jail because he's still pressed about you. What the fuck is 14,000 that's chump change. I spend that in a day."

"Momma chill out everybody doesn't move like you. We move with caution. The FEDS and the police are always watching."

"Kaniya I wasn't even about to dig in your ass, but sense you feel bold enough to speak on some shit when I'm just stating facts. You need to tighten the fuck up. Killany told me about Yirah and Cynthia. I breaded you to be the fucking best, over my dead fucking body will you let any bitch disrespect you behind your husband. I don't give a fuck who it is. If Jamal is Lucky's son, make that bitch suffer for thinking it was okay to keep a baby by your husband. Put your fucking clothes on so we can go and see this bitch."

"Momma I'm not doing it. I don't give a fuck. Yirah can keep him. Ain't shit weak about me. I'm still the baddest bitch ain't shit changed. Trust me them bitches pray every night that I don't pull up and snatch their souls I love my sanity.

Lucky ain't worth it. He wants me to do all that shit. I'm not doing it. It's not even tempting. You know why, because I don't want him anymore." I don't know whose worse between Kaniya and her mother.

I finished eating my breakfast. I took into consideration everything that Kaisha was saying. I helped Kaniya clean her kitchen; we got the kid's dressed and prepared to get our day started.

***

Kaniya took me to the Impound lot to pick up Dro's car. Fulton County did the most they towed his car, they claimed it was part of a crime scene. If they thought, they were about to keep this Bentley coupe and sale it, they were sadly mistaken.

His car smelled just like him. My phone had a little juice. Dro still hadn't called me that was strange. I had to go pick up my babies before I go home. Let me call Rodica to see if she's heard from him.

"Good morning, have you heard from Dro."

"Good morning, no because he's in the hole already. I know some people up there, and they called and told me. Apparently, after he got booked, he got into a fight with some of Snake's people, so we won't be hearing from him."

"Is he okay?" I cried.

"Look stop crying. Crying ain't going to solve shit. It's not your fault Giselle. My son is a good nigga, and he's going to protect you no matter what. I guess the word traveled fast that Dro is locked up. Chanelle dropped all of the boy's stuff off, with all of their clothes social security cards and birth certificates."

"Are you serious I'll come and get my babies trifling bitch."

"I got the kids, I'm dead serious, I guess she thinks that's he's not getting out, and she's abandoning her mother duties. I need you to focus let me say this. I've never speak on anything; my son loves the ground you walk on.

Dro is a convicted felon. Of course, the judge will try to give him a life sentence because of the gun he had on him. Do what you need to do, to make sure he comes back home to you and the family, that you guys are building together. Don't let that motherfucker testify on my son or make it to trial."

"The gun is registered. It's my gun. I know the gun charge won't hold. What you are saying ma?"

"Look are you coming over are what? Some shit can't be said over the phone. Are you're going to be in Dro's life, and raise these boys as your own? Let me know because I need to know what type of arrangements I need to make. If not, you can bow out now."

"Momma don't play with me. I need to run a few errands. Meet me at my house with their stuff. You can bring them over to my house. Their new home is with me, and we'll talk when you get here. Of course, I got them I love them as if they were my own, never question that."

"That's exactly, what the fuck I wanted to hear."

"Momma don't do me. I'm down for Dro. It's Giselle and Dro until the world blow."

"It better be, I'll see you in a minute. Grab a few bottles of wine. I'll stay with you for a few days, just so you can get adjusted to having three kids' fulltime."

"Okay, momma if you wanted to stay the night that's all you had to say. I'm not suicidal, but I'm sure I can handle it. You know you're cooking too."

"Don't use me. I'm on vacation. The boys already said they wanted some fried chicken and mac and cheese. I'll leave that to you. I'll get their rooms ready and toys situated. Do you have Netflix and internet?"

"Yes, momma I have everything you need."

"Okay, I'll see you soon." Mrs. Rodica I love her she's amazing she's welcomed me from the moment she first met me. I'm glad that we got along good. I'm glad that she wants to stay with us for a few days. I really felt a part of the family.

Rodica

I'm trying to keep it together for the sanity of my grandkids and my son, and of course Giselle. I really love her for Dro. I love how she loves him. It reminds me of my relationship with Dro's father. The only difference between Giselle and me, we had a child together when he went away. I knew what my husband did for a living and going to jail was always a possibility. I always rolled with the punches because my husband was an awesome provider and I knew what to expect from him.

I didn't want Dro to follow in his father's footsteps at all. He is his father's child, and nothing can change that. Hustling and being in the streets is his lifestyle. I can't change that at all. When he told me that he opened a store, I was so proud of him. I knew that was the first step of him being legit.

It really pissed me off that Chanelle just abandoned her kid's the way she did. Don't get me wrong I'll never make excuses for my son. I told Dro a long time ago be careful who you lay down with. Of course, he didn't listen. I could tell him how to be a man, but it was his father's job to teach him how to be a man.

Chanelle didn't even acknowledge her boys when she dropped them off. She didn't ask me did I have something to do. She had her daughter ring the doorbell and drop their stuff off. What I will say is, when I told Giselle about what happened she was on her way to get them. She loved them; the boys are crazy about her. The two of them are always telling me about Ms. Giselle.

"Grandma are we going over to Ms. Giselle's house with daddy?"

"Daddy is out of town for a while, but you two will definitely be staying with Ms. Giselle and Kassence until he comes back."

"Yay I love Ms. Giselle." The boys are in love with Giselle that's amazing. I'm sure they would miss their mom, but I don't have shit to do with a bitch abandoning them.

<u>Giselle</u>

Mrs. Rodica brought the boys and Kassence over. I was so happy to see them. I went to Toys R Us and Bed Bath and Beyond, so I could decorate. Decorating is therapeutic for me. It eased my mind a little bit with everything going on around me. I got them some toys and comforters for their rooms. They would always feel at home with me. I turned the two guest rooms into their bedrooms.

I love them, and I would never mistreat them their father has been nothing but good to me since I met him. I stocked up the refrigerator. I had a few snacks that I knew they would like. I also wanted to cook their favorite. Fried chicken, homemade mashed potatoes and baked macaroni and cheese and yeast rolls.

I made them a pan of brownies also. Two hours later, the kids were fed, they had their baths, and finally, I put them to bed. I read Lil Dro his bedtime story. I read Kassence one also and painted her toes. I don't know what I'm going to do with her. She asked a ton of questions about Dro and where was he. It finally hit me that he was gone.

I refuse to lay in my room without him. I would be okay if he was at his house, but since we've been together, we don't go days without talking are seeing each other. I wanted to cry because this is like a bad fucking dream.

Rodarius was asleep on my chest; he's teething, he's one. I poured Mrs. Rodica and me a glass of wine, so we could talk without the kids listening.

"You did an excellent job with the kids today. I can honestly say that I feel sincere about my son being with you."

"Thank you."

"I know you've been through a-lot, these past few months I've grown to love you. I'll be very proud when I'll be able to call you my daughter in law. Despite everything that you've been through Giselle, you didn't let that shit break you. You kept pushing.

I can only give you advice on what to do, but it's up to you to do it. Snake isn't going to bow out just because, niggas like him never go away. He's preying on you because he thinks that you're weak and he could still take advantage of you.

I didn't want to tell you earlier because I know that you were upset. Troubles don't last always. We don't know how long Dro is going to be gone. I spoke with his attorney this morning, and he said that things aren't looking good for him. If Snake is willing to testify that he pulled out a gun on him they'll charge him with aggravated assault. He'll definitely do some time."

"I can't let him go out like that. I refuse too. Dro is the only man that has ever loved me, how I wanted to be loved without me even asking him to do so. I'm not losing that for nobody."

"What are you going to do about it? You'll have to wait it out and see what happens. Fulton County is backed up, it'll probably be a month or two before Dro gets a court date, and right now he doesn't have a bond because he's a convicted felon they're holding him." I finished talking with Mrs. Rodica sleep was the last thing on my mind. I don't want to live my life without Dro at all. I refuse to accept this as our fate.

Dear Roderick,

I can't believe that I'm even penning this letter right now. I can't stop the tears from falling. I keep wiping my eyes I miss you. I can't apologize enough how sorry I am. If I could trade places with you; trust me I would.

I know it's only been a week since you've been gone, but I'm addicted to you. I miss everything about you. I miss us. It's killing me lying here in this bed without you. Your scent is lingering throughout the room. The picture of you and I are sitting on my dresser staring back at me.

Last night I threw your hoodie on and sat inside the Bentley coupe and reminisced about us.

Chanelle dropped my boys off with your mother and abandoned them. She hasn't looked back. Don't worry I got them. They've been with me since day one. I love having them with me every day.

Lil Dro is the man of the house. Rodarius is keeping your spot warm on the bed. It's safe to say that I've spoiled him rotten. I found him a daycare near the house. Every morning when I drop him off he's throwing a fit, I swear it's so cute. His two bottom teeth are finally coming in.

When you come home, yes, I'm speaking it into existence, the boys are staying with me.

Your mother has been a huge help. I love her, the first few nights she stayed with me. I told her that I could handle all three of them, but she didn't believe me. I miss you, Dro I can't wait until the day that you come back to me. I pray to God every night that he keeps you safe and wraps his arms around you. Jail isn't the place for you. I love you, and I'm screaming Free Dro until they set you free. Call me I want to hear your voice. I thought you said that you would never hurt me?

I love you. It's Giselle and Dro until the world blow.

Yours Truly

Giselle

Chapter 20

<u>Dro</u>

I've been caged up like an animal for over a week now. The same day I was processed in I had a run in with some of Snake's nigga. Snake was a pussy ass nigga I can't even believe that he was doing all this shit. On God he better hope these pussy ass crackers hide me because if I touch down and he's still moving around I'm killing him and I'll go back to jail, and I'm prepared to do my time.

The DEA offered me a plea on the gun. The Gun was clean it was in my pocket I gave it to Giselle, but it didn't have anything on it. I told my attorney to pull the cameras from The Main Event because I did nothing wrong but protect what was mine. I blacked out when he smacked her.

My attorney smuggled me a phone in. I only used the phone to hit up Alonzo; we had business to handle. My mother came to see me, and she brought the boys. I didn't add Giselle to my visitation list because I didn't want her to see me like this.

My mother said that I was wrong for shutting her out. I don't know how long I'm going to be gone. I promised that I wouldn't take her through anything else. If I don't come home anytime soon, I don't want her to be with anybody else. I'm a selfish ass nigga, but I don't think that it's fair to make her wait on me.

She wrote me a letter. I was surprised that I had mail when they called my name. The letter smelled just like her perfume. I had no clue that my sons were living with her. I've been trying to reach Chanelle's trifling ass, she upped and changed her number. I don't even lay hands on females, but she'll see me.

Don't ever abandon my kids because I'm not with you. It's not Giselle's job to handle her responsibilities. I appreciate her for doing that. My boys can't stop talking about her, more of the reason that I needed to get out of here and make shit official with Giselle.

***

<u>Giselle</u>

Dro has been locked up over a month. I still have the boys with me full time. I'm feeling some type of way because I haven't seen Dro or heard from him. He refuses to see me. I'm so alone out here, it sucks. I can't even get one fucking phone call. He hasn't called me once. Just thinking about this shit, pisses me off. I feel like driving to the jail right now to show my ass.

I swear I didn't think he would abandon me like this. I've written him, and he hasn't written me back. I wanted to make his time go by fast. I wanted to visit him every weekend. That's what girlfriends are supposed to do right? Niggas are always complaining about females leaving when they have a bid.

My nigga won't even allow me to do the bid with him. Rodica takes the kids to see him every weekend. He refuses to add me to his visitation list. What part of the game is this? I missed the fucking memo. It hurts my heart and soul that he's denied me that right. Each time they leave I cover my eyes with my hands, so they won't witness my tears.

The past few days, he sent me roses, with a card attached, telling me that he loves me and to be patient with him. I trashed the card, and the flowers because if he loved me, he wouldn't be treating me the way that he has.

To make matters worse, I had my annual checkup two weeks ago, and I'm nine weeks pregnant. I wanted a baby so bad; and now I'm blessed with a second chance to be a mother again. I don't even know if I want it. I'm lying I want it.

I wanted to tell my child's father, but I can't. Well I can, write him again, but I'm not. Why is he so fucking selfish? I haven't told anyone yet, but Momma Edith and Kaniya. God works in mysterious ways. It'll be all right. I always have been. I'm not the same Giselle that's pressed for man. I can do without the stress and extra bullshit. I thought Dro was different. We never had a problem with communicating

It's Friday night and I'm all alone. Rodica picked up the kids and took them with her for the weekend. I didn't have any plans. Just me and my thoughts.

Snake

Time is running out. I've been watching Giselle for about a month now. Tonight, was the perfect night to move in on her, and take everything that I came for. I knew she was home alone. I've been casing out her house for weeks. I picked the lock on her front door. Sade wanted to come with me, but I had others plans after I got my money. She wasn't part of the plan.

She was sound asleep on the couch. She could do it my way or her way. It doesn't matter to me. Money is the motive. I walked up, where she was lying, and stood over her. I smacked her in the face. She felt her face and looked at me.

"Bitch, wake your ass up. I need my fucking money today." I yanked her by her hair off the couch.

"Snake why are you doing this to me?"

"Look bitch, don't ask me no fucking questions. I don't have to fucking answer to you. I'm tired of your fucking excuses. I need fucking solutions, meaning my fucking money. You know me, and, you know how I get down. I beat bitches for fun, did you forget?

I didn't give a fuck, about your nigga being with you. I'll lay hands on you anywhere. He can't save you now. I know you were the bitch, that called the police on me back in the day. It's all good though because I'm going to make you my bitch again.

I'm going to beat your ass every day like you stole something. I'm taking all your money, and your niggas shit too. Oh, and I'm testifying against his ass, and you're going to be sitting right next to me in court while I do it. I asked you nicely the first time.

Giselle, you thought that this shit was a game. I'm not fucking playing with you. I don't play games. Take me to your fucking safe and pay me my money. Better yet write me a check for 100,000. I heard your baby daddy had it too. I know Dro got it.

I heard that nigga was the plug bitch give me your fucking bank cards and all his jewelry. Take me to his stash house, I want the work too, and the Bentley that's in the garage."

"Snake, you couldn't pull a bitch like me, on my worse day. Even if you had a shit load of money, I wouldn't fuck with you. Do what you need to do, because I'm not paying you.

I'm not the same fifteen-year-old little girl, whose ass you use to beat sun up to sun down, just because you wanted too. I sure did call the police and got you locked up.

That was the best day of my fucking life. The money that you gave me, I spent that shit years ago. I balled the fuck out, at Greenbriar and South-lake mall. It was a celebration. The same way my nigga, no correction he's a fucking boss, and my baby daddy worked hard for their money, you should do the same. You're going to have to kill me. I'm not giving it up or coming up off with nothing."

"You'll be whoever I want you to be, you're a bold bitch, but you dumb as fuck. I got the upper hand. You talk a good game, but you are still that same young, dumb, full of cum arrogant, slick talking ass bitch. If you want to die behind my fucking money; I don't have a problem with killing you behind my money.

The fact remains the same; I'll still take all your shit when I leave you here stinking. Let that shit marinate."

"Do what you have to do, again because I'm not giving you anything." I didn't even want to kill this bitch, but she asked for it. Be careful what you ask for. I'll grant your wishes. I let go of Giselle's hair and dropped her on the floor.

She fell on her back. I smacked her, and started punching her in the face, and stomping her. I'll kill this bitch with my bare hands. I didn't even bring a gun with me. I didn't need a gun for her at all, she knew better.

She knew not to fuck with me. Her life means nothing to me. Don't fuck with my money and family. She's playing with my lively hood.

Chapter 21

<u>Giselle</u>

Snake is the dumbest nigga, I ever fucked with. Dro doesn't even live here. What fucking safe? I keep all my money in the bank. I like to see it, not touch it. Free's jewelry that's my fucking jewelry. The diamonds he has I can buy a whole fucking Island with that. I wouldn't dare keep that in my house.

I'm at my fucking breaking point. I'm stressed to the fucking max. Between Dro shutting me out, and this pussy ass nigga here. I can't take it anymore. Something has too, change. I'm fed up. Today is the fucking the day; this man is going to fucking feel me. I put it on my unborn child.

This is the last nigga, that will ever put his fucking hands on me, just because they feel they can do so. I have so much stress, and frustration built up inside of me it's crazy. I'm going to release it all on him. Snake thought he had the upper hand.

I wanted him, to think that. He was feeling himself. I trained with best in Ethiopia don't judge a book by its cover. I'm tired of motherfuckas, picking on little ole me. I've been going to the gun range every day, with Kaniya, just to get familiar with shooting bigger guns. I joined a kick boxing class. Also, it was a great stress reliever. Today I was relieving all my stress. I thought Snake just up and disappeared.

I guess I was wrong; he's been lurking in the shadows all along. I wasn't thinking about him because I knew I wasn't paying him at all. Dro goes to court in two weeks. I've been hoping and praying that he doesn't show up to testify. I've already filed a restraining order against him, in case he did decide to show.

My attorney gathered the camera footage from The Main Event; we were going to use that in court, in case he showed up. I was granted the rights, to press charges and of course; I was going to do so. Dro's case was going to get thrown out regardless if he stepped foot in the courtroom or not. Snake was going back to jail because, he's still on parole, and putting his hands on me is a fucking violation itself.

"Yeah bitch, do you see where your smart-ass mouth has landed you. In the hands of a certified motherfucking fool. I told you years ago don't ever fucking play with me." I laughed at Snake. I'm not threatened or intimidated by him.

"Oh, it's fucking funny bitch, you're laughing at me?" I ignored him, and I continued to laugh hysterically in his face. It bothered the fuck out of him. My body is numb, and I'm over the bullshit. He grabbed me by neck and started choking me. I blacked out. I reached out and grabbed his shirt.

I started tagging him, in his stomach fast and upper torso. He had no choice, but to ease up. I tagged him at least five times. He eased up; he moved his hands from my neck. I kicked him in his dick. He fell back and started it holding himself.

"Stupid bitch." My back was flat on the hardwood floors in the living room. I grabbed my gun, from underneath the couch. I kicked him again. I stood up he tried to grab my leg. I jumped up and kicked him with my other leg.

I screwed the silencer on my gun. He was still holding his dick. I kicked him in his head a few times. I started stomping him, the same way he just did me. Blood was seeping out the corners of his mouth. He was holding his face. I kicked his hands and stomped his fingers.

"You think you bad huh?" He mumbled with blood seeping out of his mouth.

"I told you to leave me the fuck alone. You kept fucking with me. I was good to you. You took advantage of me, a long time ago. I told you I wasn't that same bitch; you use to beat on. You thought this shit was game Snake. I'm tired of niggas like you."

"Bitch you ain't gone shoot nobody."

"I got your bitch." I stood over him and emptied the clip into his pussy ass. I was at my breaking point; he pushed me passed my limit. I couldn't take it anymore. I was covered in his blood. I wiped my face with his shirt. I could barely see.

Lord, what I'm going to do with this body and blood? Should I call the police? He was trespassing, but then again this is Roswell, and I'm a black woman. I'm not taking any chances. Snake doesn't deserve a proper burial. Let me call my bitch, so she can help me get rid of this motherfucka.

"Hello."

"What you are doing?"

"Nothing, I'm doing some work, what you are doing?"

"I'm sick, I've been throwing up, and its blood everywhere. I made a mess. Can you come over please?"

"Bitch you ain't that pregnant. I'm not your friend call Journee and Nikki."

"Are you jealous? Kaniya, stop playing with me, bitch you're stuck with me."

"Jealous of who, you know I'm a loner. You're a damn lie; I'm not stuck with you. It's 11:00 pm. If I come over, I'm spending the night. I hope you got some food and stay away from me. The pregnancy hormone tends to travel. I don't know why my momma and Valerie thought it was a clever idea to give Nikki my phone number. I can't stand her, she gets on my nerves, and she's worrisome too."

"That's fine. If you're not having sex, you can't get pregnant. Are you fucking somebody? Bring me some soup and crackers, please. Bring some cleaning supplies bleach and ammonia, whatever else you use too.

Let me find out, you're making new friends, and you're trying to get rid of me. I'm not having that shit. Tell Nikki to call Journee and Alexis. I'm not sharing you. I don't care that your momma, is cool with Valerie.

You're my best friend put Nikki on the block list. Thank you, I appreciate it."

"Shut up Giselle. It looks like you're jealous, ain't nobody sharing me. Bitch I'll be glad when your man comes home. I'm sick of you, and all your demands. Your mouth is extra fucking smart, and you're real rude too. I'm not babysitting."

"You are not, you love me. I thought I was your Dimples, your little sister? Be a good big sister and come and see me. Fuck Dro, he ain't fucking with me. I'm good on him."

"Yeah whatever, bye Giselle. Dro might be in his feelings, remember I told you Lucky was in his. At least that's what he said. I'll see you soon, and have the door unlocked. I don't have time to be knocking on your door all night.

What kind of soup, and crackers do you want? Text, it to my phone." Kaniya knows that she can't get rid of me. She's jealous that I have a few other friend's, but she's my favorite.

***

An hour later Kaniya finally pulled up. I left the door unlocked. I hope her hands are full because she's ringing the shit out of my doorbell. She knows I hate that shit too. That's my thing; I ring the shit out of people's doorbells out of spite. It's okay I got something for her ass anyway. I swung the door open. I grabbed two bags out of her hand.

"Ugh what the fuck happened to you? You don't look cute today."

"Hi, to you too Kaniya follow me bitch." I lead Kaniya to the living room, so she could check out my handy work.

"You have to be fucking kidding me. Giselle, why didn't you say shit? Come here are you okay?" I gave Kaniya the rundown of what happened.

"Do you want me to clean this shit up?"

"Of course, why do you think I called you and told you to bring the cleaning stuff? I don't know what I'm doing."

"Next time just say Rock, a bye baby. I would've come quicker."

"Girl, I don't know all of your crazy lingo. Help me clean this shit up."

"Well, now you know. Before we get to cleaning, two questions, how do you feel after catching your first body? How did he get over here? We must find his car and get rid of it. Your neighbors are nosy as fuck."

"Kaniya, I'm not as lame as you think I am. I told you I caught two bodies in Ethiopia. I'm okay. I don't know how he got here." I can't take Kaniya seriously right now; she has her lips turned up like I'm lying, looking at me sideways.

"Whatever Giselle, don't put words in my mouth. I don't think you're lame, but you are in training. Dimples you got potential. You did this all by yourself. I'm proud of you. Go take a hot bath. I'm going to fix your soup and crackers. After that, I got five hours to find this car before the suns come up.

Damn, do you have a black hoodie, leggings, Timberlands and a ski mask? Bitch I can't get caught moving this fucking car in this neighborhood. I'll clean the body up after I get rid of this car. It'll start to smell."

"I don't have any of that stuff. I have a black fitted dress."

"You need to invest in some. I'll have to run home and come back. Do you have a tool box?"

"Yeah, you know what Free may have some of that stuff. Let's check the basement." We made our way to the basement. It was dark I never come in here. I hit the light. Free had shelves of stuff. Kaniya searched one side, and I searched the other. Hopefully, we can find something that we could use.

"I found an all-black jogging suit and a ski mask. Too bad these Timberlands are too fucking big. Free got it all. Do you have any tennis shoes, what are you going to do with this shit?"

"Yes, I have some tennis shoes. Two pairs. I have some black Ugg boots."

"Okay the Ugg boot will work, but I'm not wearing them. Do you want to help, or is it too much for you because I got it? I prefer to do it by myself, so I can move quicker."

"You can do it; I'm tired and exhausted, my body is starting to ache. Teach me this shit another day."

"Okay cool, go take a shower. I'll heat your soup up. Tomorrow will go check on the baby."

"Okay." I headed upstairs to my room, so I could shower. What a day. I stripped out of my clothes.

I cut the shower on. I made sure that the temperature was to my liking. I stepped right in, to wash this day away, and all things pertaining to Snake.

Thank God for Kaniya. I don't think that I could stomach getting rid of Snake. She gets a thrill out of doing it. Crazy huh? This past year has been crazy. I would've never thought, that I would catch three bodies. I don't want to have to kill anybody else. I'll forever protect myself, and my daughter. I guess the saying is true, it'll get worse before it gets better; I hope the worse is out of the way.

I just want to live a normal life. I don't have to worry about Snake anymore. Dro would be home soon. His home wouldn't be with me. I don't care what he's going through, don't shut me out. I'm not taking any bullshit from a man anymore.

We can co-parent. As far as I'm concerned, there's no us. I'm not even going to tell Rodica what I've done; he'll find out when he gets out. I'm not going to court. I don't regret, giving my heart to him at all. You live and learn.

I just hate the way shit played out. It's like he blames me because he's locked up. It's my fault.

I'll own up to it. I'm not going to stress myself out about it anymore. I'm done with it. I killed Snake; he doesn't have a case anymore. He can get out of jail, and he can continue to live his life.

"Giselle, your soup, and crackers are on your night stand. I'm disposing of your clothes. Don't let it get cold."

"Okay." Hopefully tomorrow I'll feel a little better. I finished my shower, dried off. I didn't want my soup to get cold. I was more than ready to curl up in my bed and get some much-needed rest. Sleep hasn't been coming to me quite easily lately. I have a feeling tonight will be a lot different and my mind will be at ease.

Chapter 22

<u>Dro</u>

Something didn't feel right. I could never get to comfortable being locked up. These past few days I've been tired more than usual. Tonight, I went into my cell early, I thought about calling Giselle. It slipped my mind, and I went to sleep.

I had a bad dream that something happened to Giselle, and it woke me up out of my sleep. My bunk was drenched with sweat. I grabbed my phone from underneath my pillow to see if I had any missed calls. I didn't. Something didn't feel right. I couldn't shake the feeling. I grabbed my phone to call my mother, to make sure everything was okay. She answered on the first ring.

"Ma, is everything okay?"

"Good morning, to you too. Everything is fine Dro I have the kids. It's 5:00 am what the fuck do you want? If you're inquiring about Giselle, I spoke with her last night she was good. Call her, to see, how is she?"

"You said she was good."

"Dro, don't be like that. I raised you better than that. She's in love with you, stopping pushing her away, and let her be there for you. You finally found the right one, and you're about to fuck it up."

"Fuck it up how? I can't ma. She's my weakness. I can't be weak right now with the position I'm in. I don't want her to see my caged up like an animal."

"Fuck your position Dro, ain't shit changed because you're in prison. Instead of taking matters into your own hands and doing what's best for you. Give her the right to choose, what she wants to do. Don't make the decision for her. Keep being hard headed, and you'll fuck around and lose the only motherfucka that loves you, and your kids for you.

If you got a woman, that's going to ride for you. No matter what you're facing, let her do that. It's not about you, think about her.

How do you think she feels, when we all come to see you every weekend, and she can't? I know for a fact, she's crying when we leave. You're wrong for that shit. If you're daddy would've ever pulled that shit with me. I would've killed him."

"She ain't going nowhere; she knows what it is."

"Keep thinking, that shit is sweet. What does she know? She hasn't heard from you. Your pride is dangerous. Dro, please let it go."

"Rodica Shannon, whose side are you own?"

"Look Roderick Shannon. I'm your mother true enough. I'm riding with you right or wrong. I never get in your business or speak on anything. I keep a lot of my opinions to myself because you're going to do, what you want to do anyway.

I'm a woman before anything; I'm putting myself in Giselle's shoes. I can look at her and tell how she's feeling. Motherfucka she ain't herself. You want to know why it's because of you. Your selfish ass took her peace of happiness. You're calling my phone at the crack of dawn asking about her when you can dial her fucking phone number and ask her yourself."

"Bye, momma. I'll call you back later."

"Alright Roderick, I love you. Keep your head up and think about what I said."

"I love you too." My mother is team Giselle, ain't no way around it. She gave it to me raw. I was listening, but I do shit my way. Man, this shit is crazy.

My back is up against the wall right now. I love Giselle. I haven't loved many females, but I can honestly say that I do love her. I know she's the one.

If I, changed my ways for her, she's the one. Before I met her, settling down with anybody wasn't a thought of mine. When I get out of here, I'll make shit right. Hopefully, time will still be on my side. If it's not, I'll make it on my side. I'm going through it too because she didn't want to go out that night. I dragged her out and got locked up in the process.

Going to jail, was never part of my plan. It just happened. I don't want her to see me in here. It's killing me to be away from her. Let's just see how this court day go in two weeks. If I'll lay down, and do my time, I'll do it. Ain't no pressure, but before I cop out on anything. Snake will be put to sleep.

Giselle

It was a little after 9:00 am, this is the longest that I've slept in a while. My body was still a little sore, but I'm good. Kaniya must be in the kitchen cooking because I smell bacon. Lord knows I'm hungry. I grabbed my robe and headed down stairs to the kitchen.

I walked in the living room. First everything was spotless. I pulled my rug back to see if there were any traces of blood. To my surprise, I didn't see anything. I moved my sofa back to see if anything was under there nothing. I lit a few candles that were resting on the fire place. I entered the kitchen, and Kaniya was cooking.

"Good morning. Thank you Kaniya for everything I really appreciate you."

"Good morning Dimples. You look better, refreshed, you welcome, I fixed you some breakfast. You have a doctor's appointment at 11:00 am. Let's eat and get dressed."

"You did all of that for me?"

"Giselle, I never drag my feet with anything. I get shit handled."

"I feel better minus a few aches. So, what did you do with everything?" I fixed my plate. Kaniya cooked bacon, eggs, oatmeal and buttered biscuits. I grabbed me a few chopped apples also."

"Girl, after I made your soup. I took a walk in your neighborhood to look for the car. It was parked three streets over. Sneaky bitch. Thank God nobody was out. I can't get caught up in Roswell. Bitch, you know it's cold outside too. I was pissed; I picked the lock.

He had three suit cases in the back; he was going somewhere. He left his phone in the car. Thank God, that shit wouldn't ping to your house. He had twenty missed calls from a Sade. I drove that shit to the chop shop in Forest Park that my little cousins Yashir and Lil Kanan owns they handled that shit.

I chopped his ass up, right here in the living room. I barbecued his ass in the fire place, you see that bitch still blazing right? Damn, he was sexy, but a fuck nigga. His dick was a nice size too. Too bad he can't use it any more.

I bleached everything down, including your shower. I used a small amount of ammonia to make sure there wasn't a trace. I called the clean-up crew to come right behind me, just to make sure everything was exactly it supposed to be."

"What would I do without you?"

"You don't want to find out."

"I can't stand you."

"The feelings are mutual. Shut up and eat. A bitch is starving." Kaniya and I ate our breakfast. I cleaned the kitchen. The fire was still going strong. I had that biggest smile on my face. I had to take a selfie, sitting by the fire place.

***

My appointment went great. Everything was fine with the baby. Kaniya dropped me off at home. I called Rodica to bring my babies home even though; they've only been gone for a day. I miss them, so much and I'm bored in this house. I don't have anything to do. It's cold I need some sun. I could use a massage and manicure and pedicure. I have a few books I could read on Kindle also.

<u>Rodica</u>

The judge finally granted Dro a court date. Today was the day for the actual hearing that we've been waiting for. I can't wait until my son is released from behind bars. I miss him so much. The kids are coming to court with me. I've been trying to talk Giselle into coming also, but she's refusing to come and hear the outcome.

Even though she and Dro are going through whatever hiccup I think she should still come to show support. I've been trying to talk some sense into her, but she's not listening to me at all. I tried to tell Dro numerous of times that he was taking the wrong approach with her, but he didn't listen at all. I think she's done with him. She hasn't asked about him in two weeks. Let me try to call her one more time to see if she's had a change of heart. She answered the phone on the first ring.

"Hey momma, how are you?"

"I'm good I would be better if my favorite daughter in law, changes her mind and comes to court with me to support her fiancé."

"Momma, I'm not doing it. I refuse too. I wish Dro nothing, but the best. I'm sure everything will work out in his favor. I'm going to Miami for the weekend, and I'll see you guys when I come back."

"Giselle, don't be like that. Please be the bigger person. Do it for me, and the kids. I need you there with me for support. If things go wrong, who's going to hold me up, and I have three babies with me?"

"Momma, I would love to be the bigger person, but I'm not. I've been pressed behind men all my life, to only get disappointed in the end. I gave Dro all of me months ago. I was open to our relationship, even though I was a little skeptical about giving love a try again because of my previous relationships.

He shut me out. I couldn't even get a phone call. He refused to add me to his visitation list. I accepted it, as he didn't want to be bothered with me, and it was over.

I'm okay though. Why would I go there today, if he hasn't allowed me to be there for him the past month? He doesn't need my support. I'm sending a prayer up for him. I'll pass. I'm tired of looking like a fool."

"I understand where you're coming from Giselle. You're not wrong at all. We all make mistakes sometimes. My son is hard headed and stubborn. I'm a woman before anything. I just hate that this little month has ruined something so great. I won't pressure you anymore. Enjoy your weekend. Call us when you land. I appreciate your prayers. I'll let you know the outcome."

"Okay momma, I'll do that. Kiss my babies for me." Dro has fucked up. I can't tell him anything; he'll learn the hard way. He wanted to do thing his way. He thinks he knows everything. He knows a lot, but he doesn't know enough. Giselle is one of a kind. She's a diamond in the ruff, she doesn't need Dro for anything. She wanted him for him.

I don't agree with him taking that approach with her because she's been through so much. She's finally finding her way back, and she doesn't have to accept what he's offering. She knows her worth. These past two weeks I've seen a lot of change in her. She's happy again, and she has a nice glow to her. She hasn't asked me about Dro one time.

These past weeks when I've taken the kids to see Dro, she didn't have one tear in the corner of her eyes.

I knew then that she was over it and moved on and gave up. I can't wait to say that I told you so. He'll listen one day; it might not be today.

Chapter 23

<u>Dro</u>

Hopefully, God is on a nigga's side today. I've been a good nigga despite my past. Today was the date of my court date. I've been waiting forty- five days for this. I've been up since 4:00 am waiting to go to court. I couldn't sleep last night. I'm anxious to see what the outcome is. I'm ready to get back home to family.

My son's need me, the past few visits. Rodarius has been throwing a fit when it's time to leave. Kassence and Lil Dro are good. I asked the two of them, how's Giselle? They won't tell, me anything, my mom either. Hopefully, tonight will be my last day in here. My attorney said that everything is looking good.

He has enough evidence and proof that I should be able to walk out here. Giselle's gun checked out; it was clean he was able to get that thrown out. The only thing that's holding me in here is Snake testifying against me for assault. The charge was dropped down from aggravated assault to regular assault; since the gun was thrown out. At this point, it's just word of mouth. My attorney was able to gain the camera footage from the main event to prove self-defense.

The only thing that could get me jammed up is Snake testimony; he didn't touch me I touched him. I couldn't let him hit Giselle and not do anything. What man would let another man hit his fiancé and stands by and doesn't do anything? I haven't been in trouble for a while. My attorney stated that this judge always looks at your past convictions. I had possessions with intent to sale and distribute cocaine and few gun charges, but that was back in 2005 that's over ten years ago it shouldn't even pull up. We'll see.

"Shannon, let's go they're ready for you."

***

An hour later I finally arrived too court, they brought all the defendants to court. As I approached the court room. I looked around to see if I saw my mom and Giselle. I saw my mom and kid's, but Giselle wasn't with them. My case hasn't been called yet. I kept looking toward the door hoping that Giselle would walk through the doors. I didn't see Snake with the DEA that maybe a good thing also. Alonzo said that nobody had seen him in a few weeks, he's been laying low. My case was finally being called I approached the court with my attorney. The judge called off my charges and asked?

"Mr. Shannon, how would you like to plea?"

"Not guilty, you honor."

"We have a witness that's willing to testify against you. Council where's your witness?"

"You honor, he hasn't shown yet. I've tried to reach out to him a few times but the hearing. I haven't gotten a response."

"Mr. Shannon, all charges will be dismissed to due to lack of evidence and no witness. I'm giving you ninety days of probation, with anger management classes. You're free to go I don't want to see you in my court room again. All charges dismissed next case."

"Thank you, sir. I'll be glad to do the anger management classes. Can you dismiss the probation? I have a business to run, and it complicates things. I'm behind with my business do to incarceration."

"You're pushing it sixty days probation unsupervised and anger management classes." I'll take that. I'm glad to be free. I can't wait until they process me out. Giselle got me fucked up she should've been here. My whole family was here except for her. The officers took me to the back. I threw my hands up at my mom.

***

Four hours later, I'm a free man. I felt good to walk up out of those doors. That'll be the last time they see me.

I put that on everything. My mom and my kids were outside waiting for me. I can't wait to get our destination, so I can pull up on Giselle to see what's up.

"I'm glad your home."

"I'm glad to be home."

"We missed you, daddy."

"I missed y'all too."

"Where's Giselle?"

"She's gone to Miami for the weekend. She'll be back Monday."

"Miami, she went out of town the day I was scheduled to go to court? Miami was more important than my freedom."

"Not in front of them Dro." I can't believe Giselle. I guess she's trying to prove something. She has me fucked up. Miami and you'll be back Monday. I'll see you Monday alright.

"Who did she go with?"

"She went by herself Dro; she said she needed some fun in the sun."

"Fun."

"It doesn't feel good, does it? You can dish it, but you can't take it. It's your fault." I'm not trying to hear anything that my mother is saying right now.

Giselle

Rodica sent me a text stating that Dro was released. I'm glad that everything worked out for him. I'm in Miami relaxing on South Beach with my feet propped up. I'm still feeling some type way, even though he's released it's 7:00 pm. He still hasn't called me. It's all good though. He can continue to do whatever he's doing. I don't have time for that shit. I'm cool on him. I find out what I'm having in about six weeks.

"Call him Giselle; you know you want too."

"Kaniya, I'm not why do I have to be the bigger person? For the first time in a long time. I'm not taking one for the team. I love him, but I'm not that pressed. I didn't cause this at all. I'm not pointing any fingers are placing a blame game. It is what it is."

"Trust me I know exactly how you feel, been there done that. Hopefully, it'll work out for the two of y'all. You have a child on the way. It's important to have your child in a healthy environment. The boys look at you as their mother anyway, since she left. What are you going to do, when you get back home? Y'all have to talk sooner or later for the sake of his kids with school and their living arrangements."

"I'll cross that bridge when I get there."

"Ugh, that baby has you so mean.

"She does, doesn't she? I can't wait to meet her."

"You want a girl?"

"Yes, I want another little princess."

"Girl, I can't deal with Jamia. I'll take boys over girls."

"Because that's your mini me."

"Don't say that."

"Let's go out tonight. I wanted to get pretty and dolled up. Who knows when I'll be able to do this again."

"I'm down." You only live once I needed this trip to clear my mind. I didn't want to be anywhere near Dro when he was released. I was making a statement, and I'm sure he got the message. I put his phone number on the block list. I wanted to let my hair down tonight. It's been a minute since I've been out. I'm showing but not really. If you look at me, you wouldn't be able to tell that I'm pregnant. I'm due in August I'll be in mommy mode.

Dro

I'm pissed the fuck off. My momma thought this shit was funny. I'm not even going to call Giselle because I'll spas the fuck out. She better be glad these kids are here, it's nothing for me to catch a flight to Miami and bring her ass home. I'll let her have her little fun. I guess she's making a statement. I charged my phone. It was fully charged. I made plans to take Giselle and the kids somewhere out of town if I was released today. She ruined that.

"Are you going to sit around here, and look like a lost puppy all night? Call her you got too much pride don't you?"

"I'm good I'm just tired. She can have her little fun. I'll see her when she comes back." My momma will not ease up on me. I grabbed my phone. I hit Alonzo up to see if he wanted to make some moves. He said he was in for the night.

Alexis doesn't feel good. I understood that. I'm bored as fuck. I wanted Giselle, but she ain't nowhere around. I logged on my Snapchat to see what's popping for tonight. I kept scrolling. I saw a snap of Kaniya and Giselle. The caption was Single Again. They were posted in King of Diamonds in VIP. Giselle looked good I can't lie. Her dress was showing off my curves. I didn't like that shit at all. It was too tight. What I didn't like was the nigga that was smiling in her face. She was smiling back.

"Momma I thought you said Giselle went by herself?"

"She told me she was going by herself."

"She's with Kaniya."

"That's good; I didn't want her out there by herself anyway." Let me log off this shit before I snap.

"I'm out momma. I'll see you tomorrow; I'm going home." It's was time for me to lay it down. I cut my phone off and headed home. I'll sleep the weekend away. I'm anxious as fuck, for Monday to get here. I'm waiting for it. I need to address some shit.

<u>Giselle</u>

I had a great weekend in Miami. It was needed. I wouldn't mind living here. Palm trees, sand, and beaches. I might have to look at some properties soon. I told Rodica that I was coming back Monday, but I'm coming back early. Kaniya's grandmother Kaitlyn had her children, and she was calling every five minutes.

So Kaniya said that she had to take a rain check. It was cool I was missing my babies anyway. My bags are packed, and I'm ready to go. Our flight leaves at 1:30 pm. I'll be home by 5:00 pm. I'll swing by Rodica's and get the kids and go home.

***

Welcome to Atlanta. It feels good to be back in my city. I changed the forecast for a few days. I'm relaxed and well rested. I miss my babies I can't wait to see them. The flight was quick, and the airport wasn't too bad on a Sunday. Kaniya and I caught the shuttle to our cars. She was headed to get her babies, and I was headed to get mine. It worked out perfect because Rodica didn't live too far from here.

It'll only take me about thirty minutes to get to her house. I connected my Bluetooth. I had a few play lists in the rotation. The traffic wasn't too bad. I finally made it to Rodica's. I could tell that she was cooking. I could smell it as I walked up the steps. I had a key I didn't have to knock or ring the doorbell. I knew she was in the kitchen.

"Hey momma, you missed me? It's quiet in here, where are my babies?"

"No, but somebody else did. I thought you were coming back tomorrow? Your babies are gone home with their daddy."

"I was, but Kaniya's grandmother kept calling, so we cut our trip short."

"Umm, what was y'all hot asses doing down there?"

"I'm not hot; you got me mixed up with your girl. We were just relaxing. We did go out though."

"Don't let Kaniya get you in trouble."

"I'm a good girl. I know what not to do. Fix me a plate so I can go home."

"Why are you running off? The kids are gone he's not coming back, if trying to avoid running into him. His lonely ass, ain't coming back through here."

"I'm not running off or avoiding him. We'll have to see each other eventually. You live an hour away from me. Of course, I want to get home before it gets dark. I can enjoy some me time. While the kids are away."

"You ain't fooling nobody get your bougie ass up out of here. Just like a nigga to grab a plate and leave. I'll tell him you're back. I'm tired of looking at his sad, depressed ass. You know I've been giving him hell. You hurt his little feelings not coming to court. He kept looking back to see if saw you."

"He'll be alright. I don't want to hear anymore. I'll call you when I make it home."

"Bye." I love Rodica she's the truth. I don't care about Dro's feelings. He didn't give a damn about mine at all. He was real selfish. I'm not even being petty. Lord knows I can be petty. Been there done that. I'm just treating him, the same way he treated me.

I can't wait to go home, curl up in my bed. I want a nice big bowl of ice cream. I'm going to indulge in a book or surf the web for baby clothes. I want a girl so bad. Please Lord be good to me. I want another mini me. Kassence will be a great big sister. Whatever I'm blessed with I'll take it, long as it's healthy.

Chapter 24

<u>Dro</u>

My mother called me last night and said that Giselle was back. I started to pack the kids and me up, and head right over there. I knew she would be expecting me. I dropped the kids off at school. I had Rodarius with me. I didn't know where his daycare was located, so I had to come by Giselle's. I didn't use the garage because I didn't want her to hear me. Rodarius fell asleep on me. I laid him on the sofa. I made my way upstairs. I heard some music playing. It was loud too.

Some people want it all

But I don't want nothing at all

If it ain't you baby

If I ain't got you baby

I stood in the door way, listening to Giselle sing. It's been a while since I heard that Alicia Keys song. Giselle was standing with her back turned. I assumed she just got out of the shower. A towel was wrapped around her body. I walked up behind her and wrapped my arms around her waist. I whispered in her ear.

"I missed you, I'm sorry. Can you forgive me?" Her body tensed up.

"Giselle." She still didn't answer me.

"I'm sorry baby. Tell me what I got to do to make shit right?"

"Let me go, Dro."

"I'm not. Talk to me please." I made her turn around to face me. She wouldn't even look at me. Tears were in her eyes. She broke free from my embrace and ran to the bathroom and started throwing up. I was right behind her. The towel dropped to the floor. I pulled her hair back and got her a towel to wash her face.

"What's wrong are you sick?"

"I'm pregnant."

"You're pregnant, come here baby, why you didn't tell me? I told you that was going to happen. I can't wait until you have my baby. I want a girl." I placed both of my hands on her stomach. I feel bad as shit, for neglecting her and she's pregnant with my child.

"I wasn't allowed too."

"I'm sorry Giselle, I swear to God I am. I didn't shut you out because I wanted too. I had too because I didn't want you to see me caged up. It was for your own good. Do you know how many niggas, was waiting to see you walk through that door, to snap a picture of you? Niggas will try to get at you just off the strength of me and who I am, and what I have.

You're prey because of me. You're my prized possession. I was already locked up because of some bullshit. I couldn't protect you from behind bars. I refused to have niggas out here lurking, trying to run into you and hold you for ransom. I'll protect my family at all cost. I'm a boss and I move differently. I'm always two steps ahead."

"You're saying all of this now, but why didn't you tell me that? I would've rather you say something, than nothing at all. I can protect myself if I get the heads up."

"I should've, but I didn't want you worrying, with Snake still moving around."

"I was worrying Dro, I was stressed the fuck out. You see Snake didn't make it court, did he?"

"No, he didn't."

"I killed that motherfucka for preying on me."

"You did what?"

"You heard me I killed him, he came here, and he tried to rob me." Giselle gave me the rundown of what happened with Snake. I can't believe this shit. No wonder I had a bad dream. I fucked up, damn I fucked up. I picked her up and held her.

"I'm sorry."

"It's all good Dro, but you have to go. I need some space from you."

"Space, it ain't no breaking up. You're pregnant with my child; I'm not going anywhere."

"We did break up, give me some space Dro I gave you some."

"Stop playing with me, Giselle."

"I'm not playing; we can co-parent for right now. I'll keep the kids during the week, and you can get them on the weekends."

"I'm not co-parenting. I want all of my kids under one roof."

"I'm not ready for that, remember you don't want to shack with me?"

"Stop playing; you've had enough space." I picked Giselle up, and sat her in the middle of the bed and dived right between her legs. I went in head first. I ate her like it was going to be my last meal. She tilted her head back and arched her body. Her moans were loud and sharp.

I missed her and this weapon between her legs, and she's pregnant. Space, she better, get the fuck out of here with that shit. I don't even want her staying in this house anymore, if Snake was able to get at her that easy. It's no telling who else knows that she lives here.

"I'm about to cum."

"Let it go I'm here to catch it." I came up out of my clothes.

Giselle

Daddy is home. Even though we talked, and made love I still wanted some space from him, he thought I was playing I was dead serious. He couldn't do anything but accept it. I'm still in love with him. He comes by every day to check on me and the kids. I'll remind him space.

It's crazy because even at night, sometimes he'll call me to talk and I won't answer. He'll call Kassence or Lil Dro's phone, and they'll give me the phone. I know he misses me, and I miss him too, but we'll be alright. It's not permanent it's temporary. I can't get rid of him. He's calling now.

"Hello."

"What you are doing?"

"Laying in the bed."

"I miss you."

"I miss you to Dro."

"How long do I have to suffer?"

"You're not suffering; it's just a space that's it."

"I'm trying to respect your wishes, but I feel like invading your privacy because you're doing too much. I want to lay next to you every night and kiss your stomach. I want to tell my unborn that daddy loves her. My baby needs to hear her daddy's voice. I want to rub your feet, and give you massages at night. I want your pregnancy to be something that you'll never forget."

"We'll get there Dro?"

"What's that's supposed to mean?"

"Be patient with me."

"I'm trying to be, but it's hard. I want to be with my family every night, but somebody makes me go home and sleep by myself. I'm sick of this co-parenting shit. What if you get sick, who's going to make sure you're okay? You have my kids brainwashed. Lil Dro thinks he's the man of the house. He's standing at the door making sure I leave when you say good night.

Rodarius is in my bed, making sure I don't lay next to you. The only person on my side is Kassence; she doesn't want to see me leave."

"I'm sorry Dro, it's only been a week. I think your handling everything pretty good."

"Giselle, and that's too fucking long. You're stressing me out. I'm a young nigga with no gray hairs. I saw one for the first time today when I got my hair cut. It's coming from you. You are stressing me out. My car is acting up I'm on my way back."

"Dro, there is nothing wrong with your car." He hung up in my face. He probably didn't go home anyway. He probably was sitting around the corner. I heard the garage door go up I know it was him. I sat up on the bed waiting for him to come up. He finally made his way to my room. He started undressing. He opened his drawer and got his pajamas out. I kept staring at him. He wouldn't look at me. He finally turned around and smiled.

"What Giselle?" He climbed in bed right beside me and pulled me close to his chest. He started whispering in my ear. I missed this, but I wanted him to sweat a little.

"Dro."

"Yes."

"Why couldn't you just act right, and go along with what I was trying to do?"

"Baby, I'm not an actor. I'm in love with you. You have my heart. I was away from you for fifty-two days. I respect you I gave you, your little space for a few days. I fucked up I should've thought about was I doing. I can't say that I'm sorry enough. I'm ready to make everything right and official. Let's put this little bull shit behind us and move on. I love you, can I spoil you? Can I lay here with you every night? Can we move on?"

"Yes, to everything Dro it's not like you're giving me a choice."

"Thank you, if you said no I was really going to wear you down. I want to buy a new house. I've been thinking long and hard. I don't want you staying here anymore. Start looking for a house; I want you out of here immediately. You don't have to sale this house you can keep it. I want us to have something together. It ain't no limit."

"I'll start looking."

Dro

I have something special planned for Giselle and the kids this weekend. I rented us a cabin in the Smoky Mountains. We're going on a family vacation I packed everybody's stuff already. Even Giselle's stuff, she knows that I'm up to something, but she doesn't know what.

I picked up Kassence and Lil Dro from school. Rodarius daycare isn't too far from the school; I was picking him up next.

"Daddy, why did you pick us up from school early?"

"I have a surprise for you guys and your mother."

"We love surprises." These kids are nosy, just go with the flow. I checked them out of school early because we're headed to Tennessee, and it's a four-hour drive depending on how many times I'll stop so they can use the bathroom and eat. I grabbed Rodarius from school; he was ready to go. It's time to scoop Giselle now so we can head out.

***

I made it to the house. Giselle was upstairs asleep. The kids were using the bathroom and making a snack bag for the road trip. I grabbed Giselle a warm rag, so she could wash her face and brush her teeth.

"Baby get up." I towered over her and kissed her on her lips.

"I'm tired Dro I don't feel good this baby is kicking my ass."

"I know. I want to take you out of town for the weekend and spoil you. Here wash your face and brush your teeth."

"Where are we going? What about the kids, who's going to watch them your mom is out of town."

"The kids are coming with us. I have everybody's stuffed packed in the truck. We're just waiting for you to wash your face, brush your teeth and we're ready to go."

"You have my stuff packed too?"

"Of course."

"You're sneaky Dro, when did you plan this, why am I just now knowing,"

"Let me spoil you, can I do that? When I want to do something nice and special for you, I'm not supposed to let you know about it. It wouldn't be a surprise would it."

"Okay, Mr. Shannon I'll let you do your thing. Let me freshen up, and we can leave." Giselle wants to know everything. I just need her to trust me and go with the flow. I keep telling her that I'm a different breed. I plan on showing her. Giselle was finally ready; the kids were ready and impatient to leave. Kassence grabbed everybody's iPad. I locked up the house and made sure the kids were locked in their car seats and ready to go.

"Giselle, give me your phone. It's about us the weekend, no interruptions. I'm taking you somewhere that phones roam. I want your full attention." She gave me her phone. I powered it off and placed it in the glove department with mine. I had a car phone in this Range Rover if my mom needed to reach me she had my number, and she could call Alonzo.

I looked back in my rear-view mirror the kids were doing their thing. I looked to my right and Giselle was smiling at me. Her smile is everything to me. I remember when I first met her in Ethiopia I couldn't get her to crack a smile for nothing.

She had her guard up, because she's been hurt. I was kind of skeptical to say anything to her. I couldn't keep my eyes up off her. I felt it in my heart that I needed to say something to her. In my thirty years of living the way I feel about her, I've never felt this way about any female.

Giselle was special to me. I'll do anything for her. My sons love her; she completes me. I wasn't looking for love, but that shit crept up on a nigga.

Chapter 25

<u>Giselle</u>

Dro never seems to amaze me. I couldn't stop smiling. He's been home a little over a week. I couldn't get enough of him. When did he have the time to plan a trip for us? I think it's cute. I'll go with the flow. I didn't mind cutting my phone off. If he wanted my attention, I don't have a problem giving it to him. I love my little family, and I can't wait until our newest addition arrives. Lately, since Dro has been around, I'm starting to feel the baby kick. I think it's cute.

Dro grabbed my hand while he was driving. I love him; he stole my heart. I can't wait until we get to our destination. I love surprises. I wonder what he has in store for me. I looked out the window taking in all the scenery. This baby was taking all my energy. I started yawning again.

"Go ahead and get you some rest baby I'll be driving for a minute."

"Are you sure, I don't want you to be up by yourself driving."

"I'm positive; it's still daylight. We have another two hours to go. You'll need your energy for later anyway."

"Whatever."

"I'm not even talking about that; your mind is always in the gutter. You see how quick you got pregnant. I kept telling you it was going to happen. I can't get pregnant I can't have any more kids. I told you I could touch places that haven't been touched I know where to bury my seeds."

"If you would've pulled out, I wouldn't be pregnant."

"Pulling out wasn't an option. The moment you slid down on it, it was a wrap. You were in heat too; you wanted to have my baby anyway. I can't wait to make a few more."

"A few more."

"Did I stutter? Of course, I want more. What you don't want to have any more of my babies, I'm not good enough?"

"Look don't use my shit on me. Don't put words in my mouth I never said that."

"I'm just saying because I'm not going anywhere. You're stuck with me. I had to get that little co-parenting shit out of your head. I want to give my children a two-parent home."

"You do."

"Of course, I do. I never had that because my father was locked up all my life. My mother was married to him, but he was never in the house. He was in the streets heavy. He never took me to school. He was a great provider. I don't remember much about him. He's been in the FEDS since I was ten years old. I don't want that for my kids. I want to be active as possible with them."

"I never met my father; I don't know much about him he's never been around. I have his last name that's it. I don't know any of his family. I know he paid my mother child support, he hasn't been in my life at all. If he was to approach me I wouldn't know who he was. You're a great father. Your mother raised you right even though your hard head and stubborn at times."

"Fuck him. A dead beat is something that I'll never be."

"I'm sure your father is proud of the man that you are today. I spoke with him a few times. I can't wait to meet him."

"You spoke with my father, when?"

"You know Rodica is my girl. He called one day when I was over there, and your mother put him on the phone. We clicked instantly. He calls me at least once a week to check up on the kids and the me."

"Damn, when were you going to tell me? He didn't even tell me that he spoke with you."

"I haven't had time Dro, you never really speak about your father with me. He's coming home in May. I'm helping him do something nice for your mother when he comes home. She needs a vacation.

I've been checking out the process to see if he can get a passport. Your mother she wants to go to Jamaica or the Bahamas for a few months.

I'm trying to see if a cruise ship will be the best option or a private plane. He wants everything setup, so when he comes home, he can take off."

"I have access to a private plane. Getting over there wouldn't be a problem. You only need a passport for customs. Why didn't he ask me, I could've had everything setup for him already?"

"Are you jealous? He didn't ask you because he knew that you would tell your mother and he wanted to surprise her. Can he spoil her? He's missed out on twenty years of her life. Don't tell her I told you."

"I am a little. I'm not going to say anything trust me. She deserves it. I'm glad that you and my parents have formed a bond. My dad is very picky, and if he's comfortable with you, that means a lot. He doesn't take to anyone."

"You know I'm that bitch, Dro. I love your parents. Your mother she's the mother I never had. Your father I love him too. He told me to take it easy on you. He'll handle you when he gets out, that's the only reason why I let you come back home. When he gets out, I'm going to be a little jealous. Your mother will be on an exotic Island, and I'll be at home big and pregnant. I want to go to Jamaica or the Bahamas too I've never been before."

"You're my queen, and you know that. You don't have to be jealous. I'll take you anywhere you want to go.

I want you big and pregnant. Just let me know when and where. We can take off. Spring Break we can take the kids to the Bahamas."

"Are you serious?"

"Yes, I have access to a plane. I'll take you across the world."

"I love you so much." I was sleepy but talking to Dro I'm not tired anymore the kids are sleeping. It was just the two of us catching up. I missed this about us. We finally reached the Tennessee state line.

Dro

Four hours later we arrived at Pigeon Forge, Tennessee. The temperature is holding 19 degrees. Snow covered the trees and mountains. I rented us a cabin for the weekend. Giselle has been talking about she wanted to come here for a minute. I wanted to come before it got too cold. I thought she would enjoy it more now because it's snowing. I stopped by the rental office and grabbed our key for check in.

"Baby this is beautiful you remembered? I wish I had a camera to take some pictures."

"I listen to you, everything that you tell me. I brought a camera. I soak it all in and make shit happen."

"I see."

"Help me get these kids out of the truck. I'll come back and get our bags." I tapped Lil Dro on his shoulder. Giselle grabbed Rodarius. I carried Kassence inside. I went back outside to grab our stuff. I've been planning this for over a month now. I paid extra to have the cabin stocked with everything that we would for, the four days that we would be here.

I wanted to stay in and relax it had an indoor pool and jacuzzi. I know Giselle wanted to shop. She looks at baby stuff every day. I'll be glad when we find out what we're having. August will be here soon. I already have two boys I want another girl to spoil her.

"Damn baby this is really nice, the pictures on the internet are under rated. I love it. It's amazing. The hardwood is so pretty, the chandelier's hanging from the ceiling. The view is beautiful. It's so much snow, it's covering the trees. The kids said they saw a bear, in the back yard. I'm hungry."

"Yeah right, show me a bear I'll believe it when I see it. Everything is on me this weekend. I want you to sit back and relax. What do you want to eat? I'm going to cook for you."

"It doesn't matter, whatever you cook is fine with me? Do we have to go to the store? I saw a store a maybe twenty miles ago. It's nothing out here."

"I had the refrigerator filled before we got here. Go pick something out so I can get started. I'm hungry myself. Which room is ours?"

"The master suite of course. It's upstairs on the right. Hamburgers and fries will be cool. I don't want to use these people's pots and pans. Let me clean them before you start cooking."

"Giselle, I know you, I brought our own stuff. Don't worry about anything; please relax. Your Kindle is in your bag. Take a shower, go read until I tell you it's time to eat."

"Excuse me. I was just saying."

"I know baby, everything that you think you would need, I have it for you. Your lotions, oils Shea butter it's there."

"Bye Dro." She's driving me crazy already. We haven't even been here for an hour yet. I just want her to relax, that's it and prop her feet up. One of the reason's I said no phones because I wanted us to enjoy each other and catch up on some lost time, without any interruptions.

I started preparing dinner I wanted to eat, relax and smoke. Maybe take a late-night swim we'll see.

***

We fed the kids put them to bed. Giselle has
Rodarius so spoiled, and I hate it, I'll break him. He thinks
that he's supposed to sleep with her every night, not
happening. He threw fit because I put in the room with Lil
Dro.

He walked back to the room with us. Giselle
thought it was funny. She finally caved and laid him on her
chest, and he went straight to sleep. He's a breast man like
his father. He started snoring quickly I carried his ass back
to the room with little Dro.

We had a fire place in the master suite. I went
outside and chopped up a few pieces of wood. I wanted to
light the fire place. It's cold as fuck outside too. More snow
continued to fall. Our room looked out to the mountains. I
pulled the curtains back; the sun had already set. You could
barely see the moon.

"I didn't know that you knew how to cut wood."

"It's a lot that you don't know about me. My
mother's father he's from Mississippi. I used to go out
there in the summer. He would cut wood in the summer, so
he'll be prepared for the winter. He taught me how to do it.
He's deceased now I was young nigga cutting wood. I
could cut fast too; he used to tell me to slow down.

I'll never forget how to do it, even though it's been a while. I still got it."

"That's pretty cool. I've never been to Mississippi before, what's out there?"

"It's country, but it's cool. They have casinos and beaches. It's about six hours from Atlanta. I'll take you out there. We can go to Biloxi and gamble, or we can go to Tunica. I haven't been in a long time.

After my grandfather died, the family was beefing something serious because my mother is the oldest and she was left with everything. My mother didn't need it because my father always made sure that she was financially straight while he was incarcerated, and of course, I was hustling. Her sister's and my grandfather's siblings were jealous. We don't even go out there at all.

"That's some bull shit."

"I know, but that's how some people do things."

"Where are you going?"

"In the living room to smoke."

"I'm coming too."

"No, you ain't I don't want my baby around no smoke. I'm only taking a few hits. I'll be back. I thought you wanted space?" Giselle a trip, I know she missed a nigga. We've had this conversation a few times. I don't want her around me, while I'm smoking. Second hand smoke isn't good.

Giselle

Dro really has out done himself. This cabin is amazing. He's so attentive to my needs. He meant everything that he said when he told me to sit back and relax. He refuses to let me lift a finger. If this isn't the real deal, I don't know what is. In some relationships when you're dating someone, they do everything to get you, and after a while, they start to change.

He hadn't switched up at all except for when he was in prison. He's giving me the real him. I hope this is what forever feels like. We're in tune with each other. We really connect. Even with a blended family, it's working out perfect. This is all I ever wanted. I've been blessed to cross paths with him. We make each other better. When I met him, I was broken?

I was wondering how I would pick up the pieces. How would I get to this point? Everybody around me was happy. I wanted the same thing. I knew God would bless me; he surrounded me with greatness. I was at the right place at the right time.

"What are you smiling for?"

"I can't smile, is it a crime to smile? I'm just thinking about a few things."

"You better be thinking about me. Come here so I can give you a message and rub your feet."

"How can I not, think about you?"

"Talk to me, tell me what's on your mind I'm listening."

"I was just thinking about us and how we met. I always wondered what's it like to be in love. Before I met you, I was always looking for love in all the wrong places. When we met, I didn't know that we would get this far. I've got it wrong a few times.

It feels good to get it right finally. When I think about you, I smile at just the thought of you. I've never been so open with a man before until I met you. I was always one to bite my tongue and never express how I'm feeling. When I'm with you, I never hold back. I had layers and wall built up to protect my heart. You pulled back every layer. I'm opened to love you. I love how, you love me."

"Keep talking I'm listening to you baby."

"The past few months, being with you has been amazing. Everything about us different, I wouldn't trade different for nothing. My daughter loves you. She asked me the other day; she said mommy. When the new baby comes, everybody will be calling Dro daddy, but me.

I miss my daddy; I don't think that he's coming back. When I call him to see if he'll pick up, he doesn't. Can I call Dro daddy too? He treats me like I'm his daughter. He said I'm his baby girl no matter what. He calls me every day. I love him too.

I feel so bad Dro that I haven't told her that he's dead. I couldn't stop crying. That shit hurt my heart before he died he didn't even acknowledge her. He watched me get my ass beat, by four women and he didn't do shit. How could you do that to the mother of your child?" I cried.

"Stop crying, Giselle. I don't want you to upset my baby. I got Kassence she's my daughter, I'm her father. We can make it official I want her to have my last name too. I got you no matter what. Let it go; I promise I'll never hurt you. I'm here now; I'm not going anywhere. I swear to God I'm not."

"She'll love that."

"You know I hate to see you cry. Your tears touch my soul. Can you please stop? Raise up and give me a hug. I love you Giselle, and I can never tell you enough. We good, you don't have to reminisce or reflect on your past anymore.

Leave it there; we're building something new together. I want to buy us a house. I'm ready to create a shit load of memories with you. It's my job to keep you happy. The only thing that I want to do is make you smile. Nothing more nothing less. Promise me you'll let it go."

"I promise."

"Let my wipe your tears and get that snot up out your nose."

"I wasn't crying like that."

"Yes, you were."

"Whatever."

"Are you in love with me?"

"Dro, how can I not? My heart wasn't even up for grabs when I met you. I tried to fight the connection. You snatched my heart the moment I let you in. People don't cross paths for a reason. It was meant. I knew Alonzo, but I never saw you with him before. You kept staring at me with your sexy brown eyes and bushy eye brows. You put a smell on me."

"I wasn't even supposed to go to Ethiopia. I could never send Alonzo on a mission overseas and not stand ten toes down with him. I was working my magic when I first saw you. I always get what I want." I punched Dro in his shoulders.

He's everything to me. I was just supposed to be expressing myself, while he was giving me a massage. I ended up letting some shit out. He was right I had to let it go. Free is gone, and he's never coming back. I'm more than ready to put the past behind me and create new memories with Dro.

We laid up and talked all night. When I'm with Dro, I don't need a phone or WIFI connections, all we do is connect. Everybody wanted to call me a hoe. The only man that I'm doing some hoe shit with is my man Roderick Shannon. Real niggas do real things. My man is real in every aspect. It doesn't get any better than this.

When you find a man that's for you and only you. It's a wonderful feeling. I swear I don't ever want to come down from this.

Chapter 26

<u>Dro</u>

Tonight, was our last night at the cabin. The snow finally melted. We took the kids to Gatlinburg; they had indoor water park The Wilderness. They had a blast. I could tell as soon as they got inside of the truck, they were knocked and fast to sleep. We had to carry them in and undress them and put them in their beds.

We arrived at the water park at noon. It's little after 7:00 pm now. I couldn't wait to get back to the cabin. I had something special planned for Giselle, even though this trip is about us and our family. I made sure everybody did something that they wanted to do. Giselle wanted to shop; we did that the first day.

The kids wanted to go to the indoor water park; we did that today. Tonight, was about me. The moment I came here I had this planned. Our check out time was at 11:00 am. I wanted to be packed and ready to go by then and maybe on the road.

"Dro, what are you doing?"

"Minding my business, can I do that?"

"Excuse me."

"It's not like that, come here I'm trying to do something special for you, and you're sneaking up on me." She followed me to our room. I filled the tub with red rose petals. I had a trail of roses in the bedroom leading to the bathroom. I had candles lit throughout the room.

"Dro, what it is this?"

"Look don't ask any questions, just go with the flow. Let me ask all the questions and you just answer them."

"Okay, daddy."

"Come on, get undressed, so you can enjoy your bath before the water turns cold." Giselle was relaxed in the tub. I started massaging her shoulders; she was tense too.

"It feels so good."

"I know."

"What did I do to deserve you?"

"You don't know yet; you'll forget it out."

"I appreciate you."

"I appreciate you too." My arms were wrapped around Giselle's stomach. My lips were pressed against the nape of her neck.

"Don't ever let me go."

"I'm not, come on let's get out. I have something else planned for you." I ushered Giselle out of the tub and led her to our room. I grabbed the towel, so I could dry her off, and oil her skin with her Shea butter.

"We're my pajamas?"

"No pajamas tonight." I knelt in front of Giselle. I was on one knee. I had the ring hid under the bed. I grabbed it with my free hand.

"Giselle, look at me. The moment I first laid eyes on you. I knew you were the one. I couldn't stop looking at you. You had me in a trance; your eyes told me a story. On the outside looking in. I wasn't sure exactly what that story was. I wanted to know more. I wanted to get to know you.

It was something about you that touched my soul. A little voice kept saying, say something to her, she's not spoken for. I wasn't going to act on it all. It's not many females that I have approached off that little voice because

I've never heard that little voice. You're the only one. Your soul was speaking to me.

When we made it to Ethiopia, and I stepped outside on the balcony, and you were already out there, I knew it was something. Your soul was speaking to me again. I had to act on it. I didn't know that we'll end up here. I've taken plenty of chances. In my life, I've always took risk, I'm willing to risk it all for you.

These last few months I've been with you, were some of the best months of my life. I appreciate you for stepping and being a mother to my sons. I'll give you an A plus for that. I'm not perfect nigga, but I'll be perfect for you.

I love hard, and I'm in love with you. I told you months ago that I didn't want to shack with you. I meant that. You're carrying a special package of mine inside of you. Before you give birth to my daughter, I'll make you my wife. Giselle Lawrence, will you marry me?"

"Yes, Dro I'll marry you." I slid the ring on Giselle's finger she couldn't stop looking at it. I'm glad she said yes. I said years ago that if I ever get married, I was only doing once. Giselle is the only woman that would ever carry my last name besides my daughters.

"Pick a date, because I don't want to wait."

"Dro I want a big wedding. Can we wait until after I have the baby? We can elope now; we don't have to wait to do that. My wedding I want the world to see me marry the love of my life. It's Giselle and Dro until the world blow."

"We can wait. I want to give you the wedding that you want. You're not giving birth to my daughter without having my last name."

"I wouldn't have it any other way."

"Can I get off the floor now?"

"Get up." It's official we're about to do this. I gave up my players card months ago. I'm ready. I want this. My life is complete. Giselle and my family are the only thing that matters to me.

Giselle

I'm so emotional right now, I'm crying, but it's tears of joy. I've been through so much in my life, I've been counted out, since the beginning. I was scared to take a chance with Dro. I pushed him away in the beginning. It was fate that I walked in the restaurant, and he was there.

I'm glad I decided to give him a fair shot. Who would've known that our first encounter, would land us here, it's not about how you start. It's about how you finish. For the longest, I've always wondered why. My life was in shambles. I wasn't living right at all.

Everything that I went through, it was a lesson. God tried to tell me a long time ago, not to do a lot of things, but I didn't listen. I knew right from wrong. The signs were there, but I ignored them. I wouldn't trade what I went through for nothing because it has landed me right here.

The trip to Ethiopia, it wasn't the best experience, but it was a life experience. I'll never forget it because that's where I first laid eyes on my husband. I went through a lot of bull shit, by choice. The moment I started to pay attention and do things the way God wanted me to do them. My blessings started rolling in. It doesn't hurt to listen at all.

I'm glad I finally decided to do so. I'm expecting, and I'm about to get married. I'm so happy right now, I haven't been happy in a long time. I'm finally coming into my own. Dro keeps a smile a face. We have a beautiful family. I love his mother and father. We're made each other. I can't wait to get back home and tell the world about my engagement. It's a celebration I'm ready to celebrate. It's Giselle & Dro until the world blow.

Epilogue

<u>Giselle</u>

"Dro, my water broke."

"Good, I'm ready to meet my daughter. Do you want to go to the hospital now or later?"

"Now of course, I'm ready to see my baby."

"Giselle, if your water just broke, she's not going to come immediately. You were only two centimeters the last time they checked you. Okay get your stuff ready and let me get the kids situated."

Ugh, it's water everywhere. Ryleigh was four days late. My doctor scheduled for me to be induced on Saturday which was perfectly fine with me. School just started back. I didn't want them to miss the birth of their little sister. I'm nervous I couldn't wait to meet my princess. I guess she had a mind of her own already.

"Giselle, where are your bags? Call my mother to meet us at the hospital, so she can get the kids."

"It's already done. My bags are downstairs in the living room closet."

"Mommy, we can't wait to meet our sister."

"I can't until you guys meet her too." My bags were already packed. I had to change clothes. I opted out for a sundress. It's been awhile since I had a baby. With Kassence they had to break my water, she was late also.

***

My water broke at 9:20 am. It's 5:00 pm and Ryleigh Marie still hasn't made her entrance. I'm so annoyed right now, I'm hungry, and the contractions are getting worse. I'm sick of the candy. Dro's in the chair sleep while his daughter is taking her precious time to make her entrance in the world. I have three outfits picked out for her already.

"Mrs. Shannon, let me check you again to see how far you've dilated."

"Okay." If they check me one more time, and I'm nowhere ten centimeters I'm going to scream. I swear to God I am. Ryleigh is going to be my problem child. I know it.

"We're making progress Mrs. Shannon you're at nine centimeters. It shouldn't be that much longer. We'll go ahead and get the room ready for delivery."

"Dro, wake up it's almost time." He stood to his feet and walked over and approached me. He towered over me and placed his hands on my face. I swear I could never get tired of looking at this man.

"I love you. She's finally ready to come? I can't wait to meet her. Just think after you give birth, I can give you the wedding of your dreams, and get you pregnant all over again."

"I love you too. Thank you for giving me the best pregnancy that I could ever ask for. I can't wait to meet her too. I'm ready for the wedding. I'll lose a few pounds first. I don't know if I want any more right now if they're going to act like this one. You have her spoiled already, and she's not even here. She knows that she can do what she wants, look how long it's taking her to arrive."

"I don't want you to lose anything. I like Giselle thick, just the way she is. You can tone up I want you to keep the weight. You're giving me another one."

"Mrs. Shannon let me check you one more time; your contractions have sped up. Ryleigh maybe ready to make her entrance." Ugh, I'm tired of them checking me I hope she's ready. I can't wait to hold her.

"It's time I see hair." The doctors came in the room. Dro sat right next to me and held my hand. I looked at him, and he looked at me. We smiled at each other.

"Don't get scared now, I got you I'm not going anywhere."

"I'm not scared, Dro. I'm ready."

"Mrs. Shannon on three give me a push 1, 2, 3, one more push on three. 1,2,3."

"It hurts."

"Come on; she's almost out. One more push. Mr. Shannon do you want to come down here?"

"I have to stay by Mrs. Shannon's side. One more push baby and it'll all be over." I pushed one more time long and hard.

"She has a set of lungs on her. Mr. Shannon, you can cut the umbilical cord." Ryleigh Marie Shannon finally made her grand entrance in the world 8/18/18 weighing 8 pounds and 3 ounces; she tore my tale up. She looks just like her father and me. She's the prettiest shade of brown that I ever saw. Her hair is full of thick black curls. She has Dro eyes and my lips.

She was so pretty I can't stop looking at her, the nurses started cleaning me up. I had a few stitches. I'm ready to hold my baby.

***

"Giselle, can I hold my baby?"

"Of course, tell your mother and father to come in with the kids, so they can meet our newest addition." Only our immediate family was here. My mom and grandmother were on the way. Momma Edith, she'll be here next week. She's going to stay with us for a few months to help me prepare for the wedding and help with the baby.

Our family filled the room. Big Dro was finally released from the FEDS. Rodica was so happy, she deserved it; twenty years is a long time to be away from someone. Lil Dro and Kassence approached Dro they wanted to hold their sister. Rodarius climbed in the bed with me.

"Momma, I don't want that baby to come home. I'm the baby."

"Darius, you'll always be my baby. We're still going to take naps together. I'm still going to lay in your bed with you until you fall asleep. We're still going to sneak off on Friday's after school to play at Chuck E Cheese."

"You promise."

"I promise," I swear this is my son. Chanelle just had him for me. He will not let me out of his site. Dro can't stand it. We'll lay up in the bed like we are now. Dro will come in the room, and Rodarius will look at him like he's not leaving. I hate when Dro makes him leave just to show him who the boss is.

Visitation hours were over. Rodica and Big Dro took the kids home with them. They promised to come back tomorrow. Ryleigh was asleep on her daddy's chest. I snapped a few pictures of Ryleigh and sent to Kaniya. She made promises to come by tomorrow to see her God daughter.

Two months later

<u>Giselle</u>

We've been planning this wedding for months. I can't believe that I'm finally about to marry the love of my life tomorrow, in front of all my family and close friends. Dro thought he was having a bachelor party tonight at Magic City. We're already married, we're just doing it, so the world can see. Happy wife, happy life I'm sorry but it ain't going down.

My bachelorette party was last week. We went out me, Kaniya, Journee, Alexis, and Nikki. We were bar hopping. I was having a wonderful time until my husband, Alonzo, Juelz and Skeet, pulled up. Oh, and Kaniya's crush Ali was already there. She knew what she was doing.

Don't ask me about Ali, i'm not telling my best friend's business. If she want y'all know to know, I'm sure she'll say something, but she's happy, and I'm happy for her, even though she's not with her husband.

We weren't even doing nothing, but having fun doing what women do. We had a VIP section. Dro called my phone a few times, and I didn't answer. He hit me up on FaceTime I didn't answer. I wasn't about to be on the phone with him all night, and I would be home soon. I'm at the bar, getting an Apple Martini.

So, somebody walks up behind me and didn't say anything. They were entirely too close. I yelled for them to backup, and they didn't say anything or move. At this point I'm pissed, and he smacks me on my ass. I turned around quick, I lifted my drink up ready to throw it in his face, and it's my husband laughing.

I was so pissed, he couldn't even let me have one night out, without him. The girls were mad because their spouses pulled up also. Dro couldn't stop smiling he thought that was the funniest shit. Every time one of my songs would come, the girls and I would run to the dance floor to dance.

The DJ threw it back and started playing **I Need a Hot Girl** by **The Hot Boyz**. We fucked the dance floor up. They couldn't take it anymore, as soon as Lil Wayne verse came on my husband snatched me up and took me to the car. He drove us home. I thought it was cute that he was jealous.

Tonight, was different, my husband was out here looking like a hoe snack. I love to see him in all white. He was draped in Balenciaga from head to toe. He went to the barbershop and got a fresh cut. I couldn't stop watching him as he got dressed. Of course, I wanted him to have fun, but I had to fall in there and cock block.

I don't want no bitch shaking her ass in front of my husband. As soon as he left, I called the girls to see if they were down to fall through. Of course, they were ready. I had a white fitted Balenciaga dress hid in the back of my closet. It was still nice outside. I paired my dress with a pair of Gold Balenciaga Chunky but Funky heels open toe. I beat my face to the God's. I took my bonnet off; my hair was bone straight the layers in the back fell in a diamond shape. I'm matching my husband's fly. He had two VIP sections two bad he wouldn't be able to enjoy them.

***

It a little after 1:00 am Dro, and the crew has been gone for over an hour. My girls and I t pulled up to Magic City. We caught an Uber because all our men drove.

"It's showtime, Skeet better not have a bitch up in his face."

"Juelz know better."

"Alonzo, know I don't play that shit."

"Ali he's good, he's not my husband."

"My husband, if he don't know, he's about to know. I don't care about it being his bachelor party, but it's about to get cut short." It was a nice crowd tonight. I could tell by the cars in the parking lot. We started making our way through the club. We stopped by the bar to grab a few drinks. The DJ was playing **Jeezy Monday Night Magic City**.

Monday night magic city throw dem grand on them hoes

Monday night magic city throw dem grand on them hoes

"Aye, it's my partner Dro bachelor's party. We got bands on demand, y'all strippers come and get paid. Congratulations, my nigga. I want the baddest strippers to come to VIP and bless my nigga." All the strippers started running to VIP.

"Oh, hell no, let's roll. Did y'all hear that shit? I'm going to kill Alonzo, Alexis. Who gave him the microphone?"

"Wait, Giselle, don't go yet, wait until they're really having fun with all of the strippers before we make a move and embarrass them."

"Okay, Alexis."

***

We approached VIP. Dro, Alonzo, Juelz, Skeet, and Ali every last one of them, had a bitch in their lap getting a lap dance making a mess. They didn't even see us coming. I know one thing Dro's dick better not be hard. I walked up and approached Dro, his eyes were low. I could tell he was good and high.

"Can I cut in?" The stripper looked at me, rolled her eyes and kept dancing. Okay, I asked the first time nicely.

"Dro get this bitch off you before I do." I caught his ass. He pushed ole girl out the way."

"Giselle, you are tripping, come here It's my bachelor party. This shit doesn't mean nothing to me."

"I don't care about all of that Dro; I know what I mean to you. Didn't you ruin my party last week? Stand up, your dick better not be hard."

"You are tripping now Giselle."

"So, stand up happy wife, happy life, right?"

"Baby, don't do this shit, in front of my niggas. You know, you are running shit.

I don't give a fuck who knows." Dro grabbed me and sat me on his lap. He was whispering all this good shit in my ear. Yeah his dick was hard. I couldn't wait to get home and ride it. Journee, Nikki, and Alexis were giving Juelz, Skeet and Alonzo the business. Kaniya sat next Ali while he was getting a lap dance. A stripper was giving her one too. It was fun ruining his bachelor party.

Dro

"If Alexis, ever pulled that shit on me, as Giselle did you last night. I'm leaving her for embarrassing me."

"That's my wife; she can do whatever. I don't give a fuck."

"It's official now; you're about to get married."

"I'm already married. She just wants the world to see. I had to give her the wedding of her dreams."

Last night was wild. It was like a movie, until my wife popped up. I thought I was tripping when I heard somebody say, can I cut in. She disguised her voice, so I didn't look up. I thought it was another stripper, until Giselle put that base in her voice, and said a nigga name. I was shook I just knew she was about to spas.

I haven't been to a club in a minute. Our new house it has everything that I needed. I'm a family man Alonzo set my ass up. I told them don't give him the microphone. I knew Giselle was up to something. I just didn't know what. She was to calm for my liking. It's crazy because she knows me so well.

I couldn't do shit, but smile. My wife wasn't having that shit at all. I couldn't wait to hear, her say I do for the second time.

"Dro, it's time." My niggas and I dapped it up. They stood in position as I made my way to the altar. I couldn't wait to see my wife. The wedding came together nice our colors were white and smoke gray. My kids looked amazing. My mother was holding Ryleigh. I can't wait to see my wife.

The bridesmaids and my groomsmen were coming down the aisle. Last and not least. My wife came strutting down the aisle. My face lit up like a kid on Christmas. She stood in front of me and placed her hands in between mine. Lil Dro and Darius stood next to me. They both were the ring barriers. Kassence was the prettiest flower girl I ever saw. I have her a ring too.

"We're gathered here today to witness the union of Giselle Lawrence and Roderick Shannon. I'm old school, but these new age weddings they have themes, and meanings. Before I decided to marry Giselle and Roderick I had to get to know them.

To know them is to love them I asked Giselle when she's thinking of Roderick what comes to mind, she said

Giving My Heart to a Boss. I've married a lot of people. When Giselle spoke about Roderick I could feel it; her words held so much confidence and power. She meant everything she stated about him.

I asked Roderick the same thing. It took him a minute to get his words together. He came correct too when he spoke about his wife. He spoke life; he stated she was his soulmate, the first time he laid eyes on her. Their souls connected, she captured the heart of a savage. He has the keys to her heart, and his soul lies within her hands.

Roderick, do you take Giselle Lawrence to be your wife?"

"I do."

"Giselle do you take Roderick Shannon to be your husband?"

"I do."

"I now pronounce you husband and wife again. You may now kiss the bride." Thank you for taking this journey with us. It wasn't easy, but anything worth having, you to put in work. You've witnessed our beginning, and now you have our ending. We're gone for now, but I'm sure we'll see you guys soon.

The End....

Girl Have You Read?

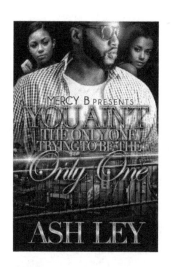